ROSÉ WITH MY FAKE FIANCÉ

A MATURE WOMAN YOUNGER MAN NOVELLA

AGED LIKE FINE WINE
BOOK 1

LIZ ALDEN

ROSÉ WITH MY FAKE FIANCÉ

Copyright © 2023 by Liz Alden

All rights reserved.

ISBN-13: **9781954705296 (IS)**

ISBN-13: **9781954705258 (KDP and B&N)**

First Edition

Library of Congress Control Number: 2023905538

League City, Texas, United States of America

Cover Design by Kate Mahon

Proofread by Lisa Matsumura

ALSO BY LIZ ALDEN

The Love and Wanderlust Series

The Night in Lover's Bay (free prequel short story)

The Fling in Panama

The Slow Burn in Polynesia

The Second Chance in the Mediterranean

The Rival in South Africa (novella)

The Player in New Zealand

The Best Friend in Indonesia (free standalone short story)

Wanderlust Resort Series

Beach Boss (free standalone short story)

Beach Resolution

Put it in Beach Mode

Holiday Retellings Series

Nutcracker with Benefits

Frosty Proximity

Aged Like Fine Wine Series

Rosé with My Fake Fiancé

Riesling with My Roommate

Prosecco with My Professor

Cava with My Colleague

To best friends.

1

Tessa

It's hard to stay mad at my friends when they feel so bad for ditching me.

SARA

You're going to have such a fun time without us! You can do all the things you want instead of us dragging you around to the typically touristy stuff.

We'll just do all that when we get in tomorrow.

JADE

Make new friends! Talk to the table next to you! Hook up with a man! You've got the hotel room to yourself tonight. ;)

EMMA

Have a glass of wine with lunch today on me, all right? I am so sorry that I screwed up my flight. How did I book the wrong day???

No! Make it a bottle of wine! That's how sorry I am.

Ah, yes. Day drinking. That's exactly what I'll do as soon as I find this tour guide. Even if it is nine a.m.

This new year, new me situation is not going well. When Jade proposed we all move across the Atlantic, I thought it would be a great opportunity to start fresh. My sister has her own family and my mother doesn't know who I am most days thanks to her dementia. Five months after my breakup with James, my circle of friends has dwindled since I moved back out to the burbs from downtown Austin where I'd lived with James. The best parts of my life were my job and my three best friends, and even though we all picked different cities to live in, we agreed we would meet up once a month.

But here I am, sitting all alone in a coffee shop in Paris on what was supposed to be our first weekend trip together. It's a busy summer day, and chatter and sunlight fill the café. I got here a half an hour before I was supposed to meet our tour guide, so my pastries are reduced to crumbs, and the dredges of my coffee are cold.

"Excuse me," someone says in French, and I glance up from my phone to see a young woman pointing at the chair opposite me. "May I?"

I perk up. There are no tables available and sitting with someone is a chance to practice my French and make a new friend. "Oui," I say, and move my purse off of the chair.

She smiles gratefully and then picks the chair up, moving it to the table next to mine where there are three other women. Oh, god damn it. I fake a smile and pretend to sip my coffee. *Nothing to see here. Not me being embarrassing.*

I glance at the women out of the corner of my eye. They're younger than me with youthful skin and no gray hairs—mid-thirties, maybe?—and effortlessly fashionable in the way that Parisians are. One of them says something funny, and all of them throw back their heads, laughing.

Great. I'm sitting alone at a table for one, jealous of strangers.

My phone buzzes with a new message in the group chat.

EMMA

Don't listen to Jade. If you aren't ready for a
relationship, you're not ready.

JADE

Who said anything about a relationship?

Tessa needs orgasms, stat.

I roll my eyes. Jade thinks orgasms solve everything. Which, to be fair, they solve a lot, so maybe she has a point, but I'm a serial monogamist. My orgasms usually come from reliable, steady partners and not from flings or one-night stands.

From now on, though, my orgasms will come from the most reliable and steady person in my life—me. Because I'm forty-two years old. If I was going to get married and have a happily-ever-after, it would have happened by now. After decades of dating and one failed relationship after another, it's clear that the common denominator is me.

TESSA

I will take you up on that wine, Emma. As
soon as I ditch the tour guide, I'll head out on
my own. I'll have that wine over a leisurely,
gourmet lunch. Very Parisian.

JADE

And then some afternoon delight back in the
hotel room?

TESSA

No. No afternoon delight. No one-night
stand.

I'll be fine on my own. I don't need a man.

JADE

No one NEEDS a man.

SARA

Whatever you do today, just try to have fun
without us, okay? Love you.

Fun. It's a long shot, but I'll try.

What I need is a clean slate. A fresh start. While I've traveled all over the world, I've never lived outside of Texas, and this is my chance. Once I get settled into Portugal, where I have a one-year visa under their digital nomad policy, I will make new friends. I will travel on the weekends—solo travel and trips to visit my friends scattered throughout Europe.

And I will not, under any circumstances, waste my time looking for a man.

The bell above the door chimes with a new customer walking into the coffee shop, this one wearing a bright blue polo with the tour company's name on it. He scans the room, probably looking for a table of four women. His eyes meet mine for a moment, and I start to smile at him and raise my hand, but he keeps going before I can wave to get his attention.

Ugh. My cheeks heat in embarrassment and I can practically feel the pity radiating off the surrounding tables. I know how to sit by myself at a café and enjoy myself, but today I just can't muster up the enthusiasm.

The tour guide is cute. Young, or at least younger than me. In his early thirties, most likely, or maybe even late twenties. He has brown hair on the longer side that tousles nicely, a wide mouth, and cheeks that are already flushed from the morning heat. His gaze lands on the table next to me, the four younger women, and he starts to head their way. I pick up my to-go cup and sling my bag over my shoulder. I'm dressed sensibly for the day in stretchy jeans, flats, and a flowy top, perfect for walking the city and enjoying the summer weather.

Paris is my favorite city. I trust it to cheer me up.

I cut him off before he arrives at the table. When he notices me approaching, his eyes light up, and he looks me over for a quick moment as an easy smile pops onto his face.

"Good morning," he says, and I nearly roll my eyes because I haven't even opened my mouth, and he already knows I'm a native English speaker and can probably guess that I'm American. I swear, the French—especially Parisians—have this sixth sense about who can and cannot speak their language.

Except I have a trick up my sleeve. I've been a regular visitor to Paris for decades—maybe even longer than this guy has been alive, so I smile demurely and answer him in French. "Bonjour, vous me cherchez?"

His smile widens, and he answers me in French, which pleases me. "I'm always looking for a beautiful woman."

Okay, cheesy line, but the teasing in his eyes brings it down on the side of flattery. This close, I can read the name embroidered on his shirt—Luc. "No," I say, "for the tour. I'm Tessa O'Keefe. I apologize, but I have to cancel."

His smile droops the tiniest bit. "Cancel because . . .?"

I paste on a fake smile. It's hard to hide my disappointment that I'm alone. "My friends couldn't make it to the city in time. I didn't know I had to cancel until late last night."

"Ah," he says. "But you're here."

"Yes, well. I know my way around Paris, and I don't need a tour guide. You've got the day off." I try to say it as upbeat as possible, cringing inside that I've wasted this man's time.

"Unfortunately," he says, "we have a forty-eight-hour cancellation policy, so I won't be able to refund your money."

I wave him off. "I know, that's fine. Of course, you keep the money."

His smile, which has dimmed upon delivering the bad news, brightens again. "If you've already paid, and I have no plans for the day, then why not take the tour?"

I bite my lip. I haven't taken an organized tour in ages,

and a tour for one, without my best friends, sounds so *dull*. There's too much pressure on me to ooh and ahh all day.

"Ah, what is that?" he asks, pointing at my mouth.

I pop my lip out from between my teeth. "Nothing."

"Please, tell me. Why not take the tour with me?"

"I've been to Paris a lot. Everything we were going to do today, I've already done, and I'm fine on my own." Those words echo in my head. *I'm fine on my own.*

Luc leans toward me, ducking down to tilt his head toward mine. It's intimate. His eyes sparkle and there's a flicker of attraction in my stomach. It surprises me, mostly because Luc is obviously too young for me, but also because it's been five months since I broke up with my ex, and this is the first sign of interest in anyone.

Okay, maybe Jade wasn't completely out of line with her suggestion.

That doesn't mean I'm going to hook up tonight, but if someone comes along who's attractive and interested and *of an appropriate age* . . .

I'll think about it.

Luc pulls my attention back to him and says, "Are you saying you think my tour might be *boring*?"

"No!" I say too quickly. He laughs. I may have been thinking it, but I would never say it.

"Please," he says, touching a hand to his chest. "I'm a very good tour guide, and there is nothing I love more than showing a beautiful woman around the city."

Okay, being called beautiful twice by a cute man is working like a charm because I can feel myself melting. Luc is obviously a flirt—must be great for tips after the tour, I imagine—but what's the harm in taking a tour I've already paid for?

When Jade and Sara had to cancel, I hung on to the idea of doing a guided tour with Emma, who had never been to Paris before. But she bailed on me this morning. Without her, I pictured myself roaming a city I knew and loved while having to listen to a way-too-chipper teenager over-enthusiastically take me to all the major tourist attractions that I tired of visiting after my first half-dozen trips to the city.

I did *not* picture a more mature, attractive man flirting with me.

"Now," he says, and he's still up close. His eyelashes are long and lighter, framing his eyes. I liked them already when he was flirty, but now that he's serious, they are even more striking. "Can you really tell me you'll have more fun without me?" He presses a palm to his chest like I've offended him. My friends' words echo through my head—*just try to have fun.* When did I become so jaded that even a stranger could tell that I was no fun anymore? Luc continues. "Me? The best tour guide in Paris?"

I raise an eyebrow. "That's a bold claim."

He grins slyly. "Well, take the tour and find out."

Despite myself, I chuckle. Who knows? Maybe this will be fun.

2

———————

Luc

WITH MY COFFEE IN HAND, I HOLD THE DOOR OF THE CAFÉ OPEN for Tessa and then follow her out onto the sidewalk. I take a right, and she falls into step beside me. It's too warm out for a hot coffee, but I opted for one anyway, with an espresso shot, because I was up late last night bartending, and I know I'll be on my feet most of the day. That is, if Tessa lets me show her around.

I was expecting four people for the tour and had a rough itinerary with a few suggestions they'd made for things they wanted to see. I had pictured a family or two couples, not a voluptuous woman in tight jeans, a perky, upturned nose, and no ring on her finger.

Looking at Tessa, I doubt I'm going to need the caffeine hit to stay alert. I like how well she's taking my flirting; that blush on her pale cheeks is enchanting, and her hair glows golden in the sunlight.

While my jobs all pay well, my clients, whether at the bar, on tour, or in my rideshare, are mostly tourists, and a lot of them are Americans who tip. I don't rely on tips since I'm

9

paid a fair wage and have benefits like universal healthcare, but every little bit helps when it comes to supporting myself and my grandmother.

All that is to say that flirting on the job always helps. And I'd be flirting with Tessa, regardless. I appreciate her concern for my time, and the way she blushed when I called her beautiful makes my heart beat harder.

Tessa's French is good but still Americanized. She's kept up with our conversation so far, so I'll stay in my native tongue too.

"Your friends," I say as we walk toward our first stop, "are we angry at them for leaving you alone today?"

"Oh, no. Well, maybe a bit," Tessa says. "Jade had a work thing come up last week. Sara's daughter had a personal thing happen, so she's helping with that. But Emma . . ." Tessa sighs. "Emma accidentally booked her flight for tomorrow instead of today and didn't realize it until she got to the airport this morning. She's got what we call—" Tessa switches to English, "—empty-nest brain," and then back to French. "She juggled three kids, a husband, and a business. Her last kid just went off to university; her husband left her and took the company. Suddenly her life is different, and she says it's like everything falls out of her brain now that she has fewer responsibilities."

I make a noise of understanding. What I wouldn't give to have fewer responsibilities. Three jobs and taking care of my grandmother means I've always had to hustle.

"Not that I blame her," Tessa quickly adds. "It's just frustrating. But they all fly in tomorrow instead, so we still get some time together."

I put a hand on Tessa's back and gently guide her around a corner. "When you wanted to cancel the tour today, what were you going to do instead?"

A shadow passes across her face, but she forces it back. "I was probably going to find a crepe cart and people-watch while gorging on Nutella, then visit the Musée de l'Orangerie —my favorite museum here—and finish the day with a nice, chilled rosé wine and more people-watching."

"That's a good day," I say approvingly.

"So, where are we going now?"

"Musée Rodin."

I hide a smile as Tessa bites her lip again. I'm sure she's been to the museum before, and maybe she's disappointed, but I have a few tricks I keep in my tour-guide bag. This *was* on the list of places she and her friends wanted to visit.

"It's a beautiful day," I say. "Not too hot yet. We'll enjoy the gardens and then go inside, and I have a surprise planned."

Tessa pushes her lips to the side in thought. "You're right. It is lovely out. And I do really enjoy the gardens. It's been a while since I've been. And the Musée Rodin is my second favorite museum in Paris." She smiles slyly.

"See? Perfect. And," I lean closer and nudge her with my elbow, "the sculptures are sexy. Like . . ." I switch to English, "man candy?"

She laughs and then mutters in English, too, "Jade would just eat you up."

"What?"

She waves me away. Then, to my pleasure, she flirts back. "You aren't worried about being compared to an idealized male form?"

"Not at all," I say and guide her around another corner. The museum entrance is in sight now, the alcove in the wall hiding the large entrance doors. "Besides, I can do many things that those statues cannot." Tessa's eyes widen in surprise as I wink at her and then greet the security guard.

Once inside, we wander the gardens. Or, I let Tessa wander and follow behind her. The manicured gardens equally hide and display Rodin's works, and sometimes I forget how lovely it is to stumble upon these masterpieces.

Once or twice, at a nude male statue, I catch Tessa looking at me. I wonder if she's thinking about what I said. From the way that the color rises on her cheeks and she looks away quickly, I think that, yes, she is. I try not to look too pleased with myself.

Tessa takes her time, especially when we get to *The Gates of Hell*, and she leans close, looking at all the tiny details of the damnation.

She tilts her head and points. "Huh. Is that *The Thinker*?"

I follow her gaze up to the panel above the doors. "Yes, many of Rodin's famous sculptures came from *The Gates of Hell*. They were enlarged and recast. The original plaster is in the Musée d'Orsay. Have you seen it?"

She frowns slightly. "I'm sure I have. It's been a while, though. I can't remember."

I check my watch.

"Do we have somewhere we need to be?"

"We have an appointment inside in fifteen minutes. You'll like it."

She smiles and returns her gaze to the sculpture, but we move on shortly. We're on time to meet my friend at the information desk, and I introduce him to Tessa.

"Maurice is an archivist who is working on an exhibit on Rodin in literature. He's also a good friend of mine and was able to fit us in at the last minute."

Tessa's eyebrows raise in delight.

"See," I say, teasing, "this is one of the *many* benefits of a private tour guide."

3

Tessa

I'VE LOVED PARIS SINCE I FIRST VISITED AS A KID, BUT THIS TRIP, and this tour with Luc, is making me think that I'd forgotten the best parts of it. I don't want to elbow my way through the crowds to see the *Mona Lisa* ever again, but Paris is full of museums, many of them more specialized and with less foot traffic.

Part of the excitement of visiting with my best friends was that I would see Paris through fresh eyes. What I'm getting instead is Paris through the eyes of a local.

It was Jade who'd put the Rodin sculptures on our list for today. Maybe it was picturing Jade's overt appreciation for the male form that had me admiring the artwork. I'm sure it was mostly that and not the cute tour guide.

The cute tour guide who arranged a very cool behind-the-scenes tour for me. Maurice, a Black man with a full head of gray hair, walks me through the staff-only areas for half an hour, showing me how the museum cares for the sculptures and how they are preparing for his exhibit and one showcasing a guest sculptor.

I do my best to keep up, but everything is so *fascinating*, and I've never done anything like this. When we pass through the guest sculptor's workspace, my eyes snag on an unfinished piece. I can see the Rodin influence, though it's a modern take on some of the sculptures I've already seen.

Even though it's not done, the pose is somehow suggestive. The way the muscles are contracted, the lean arms positioned . . .

Oh my god. It might be a man grabbing someone's hips and thrusting from behind.

Or maybe that's just my mind being in the gutter right now.

"What are you thinking about, Tessa?" Luc's voice is close enough it makes me jump, and based on his grin, he knows exactly what I was admiring. My cheeks are too flushed to deny it, so while we catch up to Maurice, I fan myself, and Luc chuckles.

Maurice ends the tour, and I thank him for his time before he bids us goodbye. Luc offers me his arm, and it's so gentlemanly that I'm taken aback. When was the last time a man offered me his arm? Luc is too damn charming. I hook my arm through his and feel that zing of attraction again when our skin touches.

Luc leads me through the streets of Paris, occasionally glancing down at me with his ever-present smile. He points out small things that have become part of the Parisian landscape—intricate carvings hidden in building facades or graffiti—and big things—Michelin-starred restaurants and filming locations from iconic movies.

Arm in arm, we cross over the Seine and stop together to look out on the water and watch a few boats pass. When I glance up, I know exactly where we are—there's the Louvre, and the Grande Roue De Paris, the spokes of the Ferris wheel slowly turning. My heart twinges. Even in full daylight with a stranger, it's so freaking romantic here.

"Have you been a tour guide for long?" I ask when Luc starts us off again toward the far side of the bridge. "Off and on for a few years," Luc answers. I appreciate him continuing to speak French with me, even though I have flubbed a few times, and embarrassingly, I had to ask Maurice to switch to English as he got too technical for me. "I don't do it often anymore, but it's my friend's company, and he asked me to fill in when the original tour guide called in sick."

"What do you do when you aren't a tour guide?"

"I bartend and also drive for a rideshare app."

My eyebrows raise. "Three jobs?" None of which require advanced education. Luc is young, but not *that* young. And then I reprimand myself. Who am I to judge? Most people haven't had a life as easy as mine.

Luc shrugs. "Mostly just the two. I like working with people, and the hours suit me. It also means I get to have a car in Paris, which is difficult for most people, and I often have time in the day to spend with my grandmother, who needs care sometimes."

"Oh," I say. "I'm so sorry."

Luc waves it off. "No, please. I didn't mean it like that. She's spry for her age, but I like to see her."

"That's nice," I say, envious that he has someone. My grandparents passed away when I was a teenager, and my dad died when I was in my thirties. I only have my mother and sister left, and we aren't close.

"What about your family?"

"My family lives in Houston while I live in—" I cut myself off with a laugh. "Well, I was going to say I live outside of Austin, but that's not true anymore."

Luc glances at me, amusement tipping his lips up.

"I live here now. Well, not here," I rush to say when I see Luc's surprise. "I'm a journalist, writer, and editor. Because I can work remotely and from anywhere in the world, I'm moving to The Algarve in Portugal."

"That is not so far from here," Luc points out, and I get the sense I've unintentionally encouraged him because his smile widens.

"A two-and-a-half-hour flight," I agree. "I fly out Sunday and settle into my new apartment."

"Only a weekend in Paris?"

"Even though it's my favorite city, yeah, I'm just having a quick trip. I'm excited to get settled someplace new."

He nods and then pulls me to a stop. "That building," he says, pointing across the street, "is one of the oldest houses in Paris."

"I believe it," I say, squinting at the facade. It's gray and weather-worn, looking like it's being held up by the building next to it. The timber cross beams give it a medieval feel. "Where are we?" Glancing around, I don't recognize the part of Paris we're in.

"Le Marais, the old Jewish quarter. Home of many old buildings and even more wonderful bakeries. I thought we would get the best rugelach in the city. It's not a Nutella-filled crepe, but it's adjacent."

This time, Luc takes my hand. The simple gesture sends a wave of goosebumps up my arm despite the summer heat. The casual intimacy is sweet, and Luc guides me to our destination while giving me some of the history of the area. Now that I'm looking for it, I spot advertising for kosher cafés and flyers in Hebrew.

Luc tugs me into an aged but bustling bakery. I peer into the glass case while he orders for us, and then we adjourn to a small local park to sit on a bench and eat. "What is this again?" I say, holding up the filled pastry that looks a bit like a pig-in-a-blanket but smells of cinnamon and sugar.

"Rugelach," Luc says, and then repeats it slowly to me until I say it correctly with the guttural "ch".

Luc ordered a variety of sweets, and my stomach growls in excitement as I sink my teeth into the rich dough of the rugelach. I do my best at the pronunciation of hamantaschen, a triangular filled pastry, and sufganiyot, a jelly-filled dough-nut, but it takes me longer to say them right than it does for me to eat them. Except for the babka, because I've had the chocolate-braided bread before, and it is much easier to pronounce.

There's a lot of moaning and finger-licking and crumb management while we demolish the box. When I swallow the last bite of my babka, Luc asks, "Which was your favorite?"

I glance down. The box that once held eight pastries was now empty save crumbs. "The hamant . . ."

"Hamantaschen," Luc supplies.

"Yes. hamantaschen. I like the—what do you call the seeds in the filling in French?"

"Graine de pavot."

"Yes, the poppyseed filling," I repeat, practicing my new vocabulary word.

"Good to know. Are you still hungry? I can get us some-thing savory for lunch here or we can keep going?"

I agree that something savory would be good, so, for vari-ety, Luc walks us a few blocks away to another bakery. I ask him to pick something out for me—I trust his culinary choices now—and sit on a bench nearby.

My phone has buzzed a few times today, so I pull it out. The group chat has new messages.

SARA

Tessa, were you able to cancel the tour?

EMMA

:fingers crossed emoji:

I send them a photo I took of the bakery treats.

TESSA

I'm fine! I wasn't able to cancel the tour, but I'm having a surprising amount of fun with my tour guide.

We just stopped for lunch. Dessert first! Look at these goodies!

Sorry, Sara. None of them are vegan! So much cheese and butter. Apparently, rugelach has cream cheese IN the dough.

We did the Rodin Museum, and Jade, you missed out on some serious eye candy.

SARA

That's okay! I did find some vegan patisseries in Paris to try. Maybe on Sunday morning we can go to one for brunch.

JADE

I'm here! Just got out of my meeting.

So sad to have missed the sculpted asses.

Luc returns with baguette sandwiches. "Thanks. I'm just telling my friends how things are going."

"The ones that missed out on today?"

"Yup."

I snap a photo of my sandwich.

TESSA

Lunch delivery. No wine, but I'll have some with dinner. Alright, back to my tour. Love y'all!

I get back a chorus of messages, hearts and kissing emojis, and I put my phone away.

"Do your friends live in the States?" Luc asks.

I moan around the bite of my sandwich. Inside the crusty bread is grilled vegetables and fresh mozzarella, and wow, it's good. Luc's eyes flick down to my mouth, one side of his lip curling up, and a flicker of heat in his gaze. I blush, and I quickly dab my lip with a napkin. Jesus, I'm making sex noises over a sandwich.

I swallow and return to Luc's question. "Actually, they're all moving to Europe, too. Jade accepted a position in Madrid for a year, and she proposed that we all move over here. I'd always wanted to live somewhere else, and I'm forty-two years old, so I'm at the point where if I want to do something, I probably need to start doing it."

Luc nods. "And the others?"

I bite off more of my sandwich and chew and swallow before answering. Here I am, sitting in one of the most beautiful cities in the world, eating a simple yet delicious sandwich while sitting in the shade of a tree on the streets of Paris. It feels everyday, and yet not.

"Sara was absolutely not going to come to Europe. She has one daughter, Zoe, in college, and they are inseparable. But then Zoe applied to study abroad in Munich, and they accepted her for a program that starts next week. Sara's a yoga instructor and teaches online lessons since COVID, so she is moving to this cute German spa town—close to Munich but not too close—and focusing on her business. That's actually how we all met; at Sara's yoga classes. Then we started going to a nearby wine bar afterward, and now it's been a decade of friendship."

Luc's eyes crinkle at the corners. "Yoga and wine."

I laugh and pull an errant strand of my blonde hair out of my face and tuck it behind my ear. "I know, so bougie. I still do yoga with Sara, but Emma never attended all that regularly because she was too busy, and Jade often traveled for work. Anyway, the last of our group is Emma, and I thought there was no way she was going to come. She'd never even had a passport. But she's divorced and her three kids are off at school and they helped us *convince* her to find a business school to attend to finally get her MBA."

Luc exaggerates a thoughtful face, his thin lips canting to the side. "All right, I forgive them for abandoning you."

I laugh. "I forgive them, too. They are pretty great, and it's fine. I don't mind being by myself."

"You don't have a boyfriend or partner?"

Talking about my ex is a lot less fun than talking about my best friends. "I broke up with someone five months ago. Or, well, he dumped me." My sandwich is gone now, so I crumple up the paper wrap and hold it in my lap, the corners poking the soft skin of my palm. I wasn't just dumped. James dumped me for a younger woman. I saw photos on James' Instagram before I unfollowed him. The reminder is like a cold dump of water over me. Age-appropriate women for Luc are probably in their twenties.

"He didn't deserve you," Luc says. It's a kind thing to say. Luc is a sweet guy, and it's a good reminder that there are nice men out there. It's just too bad that the ones in their forties are probably not single.

"Well, thank you, but I thought he did. I thought . . . well, I thought he was going to propose. We'd talked about it, and I had this silly idea that he would propose at the Eiffel Tower."

I flush, embarrassed that at my age, I wanted something so cheesy, but I did. I wanted the romance of Paris. No one had ever proposed to me before, and I thought finally I'd found the one.

Sometimes, I think what I am actually mourning in my breakup with James is the death of the hopeless romantic in me.

In this sense, I wish I could be more like Jade. She never married and never wanted to. She's had a few serious relationships, but no breakup has ever broken her heart.

Or perhaps she just guards her heart too well.

"Ah," Luc says, turning to me and placing his arm on the backrest behind me. "A little cliché, yes?"

"A little dumb. The Eiffel Tower is dumb." I'm so indignant that Luc laughs. "What? It's true. Its value is purely in tourism, and it just cements this nebulous idea that Paris is the city of love, which is ridiculous. Paris can be just as unromantic as any other city. There are moments of love and heartbreak everywhere. A romantic gesture here is just disguised because it's actually unoriginal and cliché."

"Or any other city can be just as romantic as Paris."

When I glare at him, he winks at me, easing the sting of his counterpoint. "You've grown up here, right?" I ask. "Surely, you're tired of the tourists and the pressure of romance."

"I'm sorry to disappoint," he says, and his hand cups my shoulder, squeezing. "I still believe in romance and love."

I open my mouth to argue that I never disparaged love, but the words don't come out. Do I still believe in love? Or have I become cynical even in that? There's a difference in believing that love exists and believing that love exists *for me*.

Instead of answering, I stand. "Time to go?"

At Luc's nod, I toss my balled-up paper into the trash, ready to move on from thinking about my loneliness.

4

Luc

I SHOULD HAVE BEEN LETTING TESSA LEAD ME AROUND PARIS this whole time because the view from behind is fantastic. The jeans she wears are tight and stretchy, hugging her ass. She's got a beautiful figure—petite on top, generous on the bottom.

She glances back at me and holds out her hand. I lazily let my gaze wander up before reaching out for her hand and catching up to walk by her side. The corner of her mouth quirks up into a smile.

While I never would have called myself romantic, I certainly am compared to Tessa. My heart aches hearing the pain in her voice, the way she tries to brush off her history and pretend that she's fine.

Someone should remind her how it feels to fall in love.

Our next stop is the Victor Hugo Museum, and Tessa pauses outside the door and asks, "Did I mention that my degree is in English Lit?"

"No. Have you been here before?"

She shakes her head, and I lead her up the stairs. I'm still holding her hand, which I have never done with another tour group. This tour for one is intimate and comfortable. We feel like a couple.

When Tessa told me she was moving to The Algarve, I said that it wasn't that far. Tessa thought I meant for her flight from here, but I was thinking *if I wanted to see her again.* I do *not* need to be having ideas like that, especially when Tessa is so far out of my league. The surprise in her voice when she found out I work three jobs would be enough, but it's also in her dress and her mannerisms. Her bag is designer, her earrings are, I'm pretty sure, real diamonds, and even her pants are nicer than anything I've owned, with a cut that compliments every curve.

She makes me think of old photos of movie stars: classic and timeless beauty.

When my brain isn't thinking about her being classy, it's thinking much dirtier thoughts. Throughout the day, Tessa's smile has grown, and she's added a little more swagger to her walk. The woman I first saw at the café, alone and sad, trying to get out of our tour, is not the same woman I have now.

We spend an hour in the museum, no backstage pass this time, and learn about the life of the famous writer, including the many talented people of Hugo's time that were entertained here and the facets of Hugo's life most people don't know about, like his own art and decorating. Tessa enjoys herself so much I am loath to pull her out, but I know she'll like our final stop even more.

When we arrive, Tessa glances up at the bookstore's sign. "You know, I didn't pack many books to bring with me to Europe."

"I thought that might be the case."

She side-eyes me. "This could be dangerous. You may have to help me carry books back to the hotel."

"We can take a car if you'd prefer."

Her mouth twists to the side, and there's a twinkle in her

eye. "Let's see what kind of damage I can do," she says as she steps into Shakespeare and Company. An hour later, we emerge, laden with two bags of books.

"You enjoyed yourself," I remark.

Tessa slumps onto a nearby bench, the bags hitting the ground. "I trimmed it down," she pants, "by at least half."

She picked out books for herself—a contemporary memoir and two classic novels—and books for her friends—a vegan cookbook, two business books, and a handful of modern novels. "I can't believe there were no romance books. I was hoping to find a series we could all swap around every time we see each other."

When the books are back in the bags, I take a bag from her. "Do you want to walk or hire a car back to your hotel?" I ask.

Tessa glances up at the sky. Although sunset is still a couple of hours away, it's starting to cool slightly. The shadows are elongating, and office workers are out on the streets.

"Would it be terrible to walk?" she asks.

"Not at all."

Her hotel is in Saint-Germain-des-Prés, and we've done a loop in the city. I'm still pointing things out to her as we go, sharing whatever tidbits of information I have that I think she might enjoy, although her responses are quieter as we near the hotel.

"Have you stayed here before?" It's a boutique hotel, small and modern, located right on Saint-Germain. Liveried staff open the doors for us.

"Yes, every time I come here. It's almost nostalgic now."

Tessa leads the way over to a seating area and puts her bag of books down. I put the other bag next to hers, and Tessa fans the collar of her top. This is the end of the tour. My responsibilities are over, but I don't want to go. Tessa's friends don't arrive until tomorrow, and I can't bear the thought of leaving her alone.

"Tessa," I begin.

"Holy shit," she mutters under her breath, eyes wide at something over my shoulder.

"Who? What's wrong? What is it?"

"I really thought I would never see him again." She turns and tugs my hand, trying to walk in the opposite direction, completely forgetting about the bags of books at our feet, until a voice calls out from behind me. A man's voice.

"Tessa?"

She freezes and then spins on her heel. Her eyes are wide, her grip on my hand tight. I give her a squeeze and turn around, too. There's a white American man walking away from the bar of the hotel. An Asian woman perches at one of the barstools he just vacated, watching him walk toward us.

He's sharply dressed, fitting in perfectly at the hotel, while my polo shirt and khakis are out of place. The woman he left behind has a severe haircut, black clothes, and wears a lot of jewelry. They both look well-put-together and wealthy; her purse is a brand I recognize, not the same as Tessa's. "James," Tessa says in greeting, an undercurrent of tension in her words. She'd mentioned a James, hadn't she?

"Fancy seeing you here," the guy says, waving for his partner to join us. She gracefully gets to her feet and follows him, her jewelry catching the light and making her sparkle. James holds his arms out for a hug as his partner joins us. Tessa reluctantly accepts the hug with one hand, awkwardly patting him on the shoulder.

"It is my favorite hotel in Paris," Tessa says.

"And I have you to thank for introducing me to it," he responds.

The guy's attention turns to me, and his gaze zeros in on our hands, which are still tangled together. "Who is this?" he asks, eyes narrowing.

Tessa looks down at our joined hands and then glances up at me. There's a moment of hesitation, and I smile at her.

The grin she returns is mischievous. Her hand relaxes, letting go of mine, and Tessa's arm slides around my back to grip my waist, her other hand coming up to my chest. I return the embrace, wrapping my left arm around her shoulders, but instead of cupping her, I let my palm sit at the junction of her neck and shoulder. James's eyes zero in on my hand.

"This is Luc," Tessa says.

"A tour guide?" James' attention is on my shirt now, where the company logo sits. His lips curl up in a sneer like he's judging her for being on a guided walk of the city or judging me for my job.

"Well—" Tessa starts, but I interrupt in French.

"Tessa's far beyond the need for a tour guide in Paris. She's practically a local."

He glares at me. "We don't speak French."

I pretend to be embarrassed and switch to English. "Oh, I'm so sorry. I was just saying, Tessa doesn't need a tour guide. She *is* so fluent and familiar with the city." I look down at Tessa, and she's already flushed from the compliment, so I squeeze lightly with my fingers. Her reaction distracts me; her eyelids flutter, and her body shudders against mine.

Interesting.

A throat clears, and I break eye contact with Tessa. I offer a hand to James.

He takes my hand, and the handshake is so typical of a guy with money, I almost laugh; a firm grip as if to put me in my place beneath him. James glares at me when our hands drop, and I'm clearly not forgiven for pointing out that they're the ones dealing with a language barrier, not Tessa.

It's petty, but if one were keeping score, I'd be winning.

I don't like this guy, and I can't believe that us running into him is that big of a coincidence, but I feel the need to stand up for her, stake my claim over her and wipe the smirk off this moron's face.

The woman at James's side clears her throat, and James introduces us. "Tessa, Luc, this is Yumi."

Yumi offers her hand to Tessa and smiles. "I've heard a lot about you." I can't tell if that's a good thing or not.

And then James just *has* to open his mouth again. "Yumi is my girlfriend."

Yumi nudges him, eyes wide, and James laughs. "Oh, right. You're the first ones to hear. She's not my girlfriend. She's my fiancé now."

Tessa, who had relaxed against me somewhat, stiffens again.

They don't notice, and Yumi tosses her straight black hair with a flick of her chin and holds out her left hand, showing off an enormous diamond ring. "He just proposed today! At the Eiffel Tower." She gazes up at James with fluttering eyelashes, but James is watching Tessa. Us bumping into them cannot be a coincidence; it's calculated to rub their engagement right in Tessa's face. This is one of those things I'll never understand about human nature. How can someone intentionally hurt a person as sweet as Tessa?

Tessa doesn't react, but with all the discussion today about romantic gestures and the city of love, Tessa's got to be hurt. She obliges social conventions and leans in to admire the ring. "It's beautiful," she says, and Yumi and James preen. Despite the situation, I feel like laughing because even though I've only known Tessa for the better part of the day, I know she's lying. She's smiling, but it's fake, and James and Yumi are too self-absorbed to notice. "This isn't your grandmother's ring, though," Tessa comments.

"Oh, no. Yumi would never settle for that thing," he laughs.

Tessa doesn't flinch at the insult. I wonder how Tessa knows what his grandmother's ring looks like. Perhaps they'd looked at it together, planning their future.

Beneath my hand, I feel Tessa brace herself. "Were you

surprised?" she asks Yumi. Tessa is so achingly polite when all I want to do is punch James.

"Oh yes," Yumi responds, flipping her hair again. "I mean, yes, but also, no. People are going to say that it's too soon. But, like, when you know, you know. Honestly, it doesn't matter how long it's been when you find your perfect match."

There's a moment of dead air, and Yumi has the audacity to try to console Tessa. "Plenty of women get married for the first time at your age."

Tessa smiles, or bares her teeth, I can't tell which. "I kind of hate her," Tessa mutters in French under her breath. I grin, and it's not fake at all. I like this development.

Tessa's clearly hurt, and James is so *smug*, but I've got an idea.

I whisper to her in French, "What do you say we burn bridges and go down in–what does Bon Jovi say? A blaze of glory?"

She eyes me, a flicker of amusement on her face.

I squeeze Tessa closer to me, and say, in English, to James and Yumi, who've been watching us with more and more irritation, "It's a shame you didn't take advantage of the fireworks last night like I did."

Yumi's brows clinch together. "What do you mean?"

"Well," I say, looking at Tessa with as much affection as I can—not having to fake it all that much, to be honest. She looks at me, confused, but something in my grin—mischief, I would guess—has her slowly grinning back at me. "I proposed last night under the fireworks. You know, they do that show in the summer where the tower lights up and then the pyrotechnics start."

Tessa coughs to hide a laugh as both James and Yumi look at us in shock. "But," Yumi flusters, eyes darting down to look at Tessa's hands. "Where's your ring?"

"Oh," I say. "My grandmother begged me to use her ring to propose. She just loves Tessa so much. And who doesn't?" I say with a chuckle. "Can you believe my grandmother was so excited to give Tessa the ring her mother hid in a loaf of bread when she escaped Nazi Germany?" That part's true. "Of course, it's not the same diamond anymore. My grandad replaced it with a bigger one in the sixties." That part isn't true. "Anyway, the ring doesn't quite fit right. It needs to be resized, so we thought it best not to walk around Paris with something so important if it might slip right off her finger."

James and Yumi stare at us, so I just keep rolling. I'm good on my feet, as many of my jobs require. "We can certainly relate to people thinking it's quick. You are so right, Yumi." I emphasize this by squeezing Tessa's shoulder. I look down at her and find that I don't have to lie with this part. "When you know, you know."

I speak to Tessa in French. "How long have we been dating, my darling?" I say it warmly and bend my head down to nuzzle her.

Tessa answers, also in French. "Hmmm . . . four months? Just after James and I broke up, that sack of shit."

I throw my head back and laugh, switching back to English. "We've been together four months, and I just know she's the one." I shrug like I can't help falling in love with her.

Yumi frowns, but I don't let her speak.

"James, Yumi, it was lovely to meet you, but I must sweep my future bride off her feet this evening while we celebrate our engagement at dinner. Last night we were too busy cele-brating in a different way." I wink at James, and he glowers. I bend over, picking up both bags of books in one hand and then slinging my other arm over Tessa's shoulder, guiding her away from her ex.

"Au revoir," Tessa calls with a wave and keeps talking in French. "Good luck dealing with his mother. I bet she hates you, and that's why you don't have his grandmother's ring!"

Tessa threads her fingers through mine at her shoulder, and we can barely contain ourselves as we walk away. Once we round the corner to the elevators, Tessa launches herself at me.

I laugh and drop the books, wrapping my arms around her waist, her exuberance overwhelming. She kisses my face all over, lips included, and I'm so shocked I squeeze her harder, so I don't drop her. "Thank you, thank you, thank you. That was amazing! James was such a smug little shit, he totally deserved to be put in his place." She slides down, still laughing, and rests her forehead on my chest. Her grip on my shirt is tight, and I'm just glad she's breathless with laughter instead of heartbroken.

5

Tessa

OH MY GOD, OH MY GOD, OH MY GOD. ONE-UPPING JAMES FELT so freaking good. Cathartic. Yes, it sucks that he's marrying her, but it was so satisfying to see his little bubble pop.

Luc was perfect. So perfect. He was warm and affectionate and knew right where to hit James.

I was also a bit shocked that James proposed with a ring that wasn't his grandmother's. I remembered the day, a year ago, perhaps, when James' mom, Veronica, had pulled me into her husband's office and opened the safe. "This ring has been in our family for four generations. Originally it was my great-grandmother's, and she was a Vanderbilt," she told me. "Someday, James will give you this ring, and then you'll be the daughter I always wanted." She had squealed with delight, and the ring was beautiful, and I was so in love with James at the time.

Lying about my relationship with Luc was so petty, but it felt so good. Being dumped by James made me feel power-less, and here I was, reclaiming some power back. All because I had Luc by my side.

The elevator dings, and Luc holds my shoulders, turning me around and guiding me in. I'm still laughing as I press the button for my floor.

"I'm sorry," I say, pulling out my phone and waving it. "I *have* to text my friends and tell them." Luc grins and leans against the wall.

TESSA

James is engaged. Just ran into him in the hotel. He proposed at the EIFFEL TOWER.

JADE

That fucker!

He seriously proposed to her? What a home-wrecker.

SARA

Oh hon, I'm so sorry.

Jade, how do you know she's a home-wrecker? They could have met after the breakup.

JADE

Come on, Sara. James would totally do that.

I mean, in retrospect, it is something he would do. You know we didn't know, Tessa.

TESSA

I know.

EMMA

He MUST have known you were in Paris. And staying at your favorite hotel? Come on.

SARA

How though?

JADE

I don't know, but if it looks like shit, smells like shit, tastes like shit . . .

EMMA

Ew.

God, I wish I hadn't fucked up my travel.
Tessa, I can't believe you have to be alone
right now!

TESSA

Oh, I'm not alone.

Plot twist: I have acquired a fiancé in the
form of our tour guide.

JADE

YESSSSS. I like where this is going.

TESSA

He was so great! Luc was perfectly
affectionate and he totally one-upped James'
proposal. You should have seen James' face.

Does that make me an awful person?

JADE

NO! James is the awful person.

SARA

He deserves it.

JADE

Sara has spoken.

I look up, realizing that we've stopped. Luc had guided me out of the elevator and to the hallway on my floor, waiting patiently with laughter in his eyes. When we were down-stairs, he'd looked at me like that, too, warm and affectionate. This time, though, there's no one to witness it, and it's just for me.

"Sorry," I say, waggling my phone in the air and talking in English. "My friends have *opinions* about James' new relation-ship status."

"That is okay," he responds.

"Thank you again. That was . . ." I was in such a high after the confrontation that *now* I remember leaping into Luc's arms. "Oh my god, Luc! I kissed you!" I put my hands over my face, which flares hot with embarrassment, and of course, my phone is in one hand, so I whack my eyebrow with it and wince.

"It is fine, totally fine." He pulls me in for a hug, and I remember why it's so easy to be overly affectionate with him. He feels good.

My phone pings in my hand, and Luc pulls away. "We are engaged," he teases me. "It's a perk of the position. You can kiss me anytime you want."

If my cheeks could get any redder, they would. I look at my phone and see another message in our group chat.

JADE

Are you going to bang the tour guide? He did rescue you.

A laugh bursts out of me, and I can't help but channel Jade and flirt back. "Are there other perks?" I meant for it to land like a joke, but it's breathy instead.

Luc's smile widens and turns rakish. My laughter fades, and we look at each other in a heavy silence. Luc could make a joke or change the subject, but he doesn't. "Let me take you to dinner."

"Really?" I say, with more surprise in my voice than there should be. We went from flirting to actually going on a date?

Luc checks his phone. "It is early now, but people watching and a cold glass of Rosé was on your itinerary, and I have just the place in mind. But I do have to be at work in a few hours."

Oh, right. It's not a date, because Luc has to work and I'm just a job. Even if he hadn't been my tour guide, I'm still just passing through.

Plus, the age difference.

Yeah. Not a date.

I realize Luc is still holding two heavy bags of books. "Oh, um." I glance at the signs on the wall. "This way."

Luc lingers inside the door of the hotel room while I put my books down and use the restroom to freshen up.

I hesitate, hand hovering over my purse, and decide to get this out of the way. I pick out a few bills. "Luc," I say, and his attention moves from his phone to me. "Before dinner, I just wanted to say thank you for the tour." I step toward him and hold out the money. "Here's the deal. You take this money, and your tour guide job is over. We'll go to dinner as . . ." It's not a date, so I finish with, "friends."

Luc thinks about it for a moment and then takes the well-earned money. "Deal. Though technically, I believe I'm your fiancé." He winks.

I pretend to shake my head in annoyance, but the smile I can't hide negates it. He insists I don't need to change clothes, so in a few minutes, we're headed back down in the elevator. In the lobby, I look around for James and Yumi, but thankfully they're gone.

Luc leads the way, and soon we settle into a bistro with tables outside. My purse goes in the third chair, and Luc orders for us; a bottle of rosé and some canapés.

"You'll miss your friends, won't you? You won't see them as often as you did back in the States," Luc says, raising his chin at my purse and the phone inside.

"We won't see each other as often, but we text and video chat almost every day. We all committed to getting together once a month for a weekend. This time it's Paris, and before we leave here, we'll pick a weekend and place for next month."

Our wine comes, and the server pours our glasses. It's crisp and light, so refreshing and perfect for a summer evening.

I groan in appreciation. "My third visit to Paris was with my grandmother," I tell Luc. "I was twenty, and we went to Aix-en-Provence with a tour group, and we drank wine at every lunch and dinner. Even though I drank in college, I thought it was so cool and sophisticated. I drank a *lot* of Rosé that trip."

Luc takes a sip and hums in approval too. "Were you close to your grandmother?"

I shook my head. "Not really. We fought during the trip. She was uptight, and at twenty, I didn't like the restriction she tried to put on me. She didn't drink at all, actually."

"Sounds pretty different from my grandma. Mine is old-school French, a bottle of table wine with every meal and cigarettes after."

"And your parents?" I ask. He is obviously fond of his grandmother, but he hasn't mentioned his mom or dad.

"My father was never in the picture, and my mother left when I was young. Mémé didn't always have an easy time raising me. It's better now. She's doing marvelously for being in her seventies, and she just might live forever. Her mother lived to be ninety-two."

"Do you have a girlfriend? Or a real fiancé?"

"No, I'm alone," Luc says with an eyebrow raise, and I think about how a flirt like Luc probably brings home women or girlfriends. He changes the subject. "You said you are a writer, journalist, *and* editor?"

"I run a travel magazine. I started out writing, but now I'm the boss. I've spent my whole life traveling and have always loved it."

"When you travel like this," Luc gestures, as if to encompass all of Paris, "is it work or pleasure?" There's a bit of that tease in the question again.

"This weekend is all pleasure," I say, and Luc leans closer. The heat in his gaze causes the flirty chemistry to tip over into sexual tension, butterflies and heat flickering in my core. I have the hotel room to myself tonight, and I haven't been with anyone since James. If Luc didn't have to work tonight, would I want to give myself a treat in the form of a younger, flirty man in my bed? Am I even capable of a one-night stand?

Our food comes, and we fall into easy chatter. Luc asks about my other trips to Paris, and when I tell him about visiting during the Euro Championship, it leads to talk about European football.

The food is good. We keep ordering little dishes, another bottle of wine, and the streets slip into darkness.

"What will you do tomorrow?" Luc asks, leaning in close. My stomach flips at the way he smells and how I can see the long, thick eyelashes he has. Even though they are pale golden, fairer than his hair, they catch the light and frame his eyes.

"The rest of the group gets in tomorrow morning. Once they had to reschedule, they coordinated to meet at the train station and then come to the hotel. I imagine we'll grab breakfast at the restaurant and then go do all the things that were on our list for today."

"Busy day then."

I grin. "I don't suppose you are free . . . to play tour guide tomorrow?"

Luc laughs, clearly expecting me to end the sentence a different way. "No, I have to work at the bar. But if you give me your number, I can text you some tips."

We swap numbers, and Luc checks his watch. "I better get going. My shift starts soon." He starts to pull out his wallet, and we wrestle for a few minutes, me refusing to take any money from him. "I picked the place," he says. "And this will cover the rest of the wine that you can enjoy while people watching now."

"I don't care."

"If you pay, this won't be a date."

"That's sexist bullshit," I say instead of pointing out that it's not a date regardless, and he laughs and then grabs my outstretched hand that's trying to shove the cash back into his pocket.

"Please," he says, sobering his tone. "I feel bad that you had to pay for a full tour when it felt more like a date. An all-day date." His grin is back.

"Fine," I huff. "But you really don't need to feel bad. I had a great time today, and it was worth every penny."

"Well then, I have a clear conscience." He slips the cash under his plate and picks up the wine bottle, pouring a generous glass of Rosé for me and emptying the bottle.

When he's done, I stand, and Luc smiles, but it's tinged with sadness. "It was a pleasure meeting you, Tessa." He opens his arms, and I give him a hug.

"Thank you for being my fake fiancé," I say into his chest and am rewarded by feeling his chuckle.

I let go—reluctantly—and Luc steps away, giving me a wave before he turns and threads his way out of the café. I sit and, once he's out of view, slump down, propping my chin up with my hand.

He's just a guy, I tell myself. *A guy who you'll never see again.*

I pick up my wine and take a sip, the refreshing drink rolling around on my tongue before I swallow.

Alone again.

But not for long. My friends are on their way.

I pull out my phone and see a string of new messages, starting with:

JADE

I bet they're banging right now.

The conversation moved on when I didn't answer. There are messages swapping travel information for the morning, Sara sending us a picture of her and her daughter in her new dorm room, and Emma complaining about the hostel she has to stay in tonight because she had to scramble to book a room when she messed up her travel schedule. I type an update.

TESSA

No banging the tour guide. Luc had to work tonight, which is probably for the best.

JADE

You mean, no banging your FAKE FIANCE!

And not for the best. Lack of orgasms are never "the best."

TESSA

I don't think you realize how young Luc is.

JADE

There is a line of what's acceptable and what's not, but I highly doubt you would be attracted to a barely legal kid.

EMMA

What is the line?

How young would you date, Jade?

The messages that ensue are an age gap debate. Jade insists that as we get older, a bigger age gap is fine, but I'm not so sure. Emma and Sara both balk at anyone remotely close to their kids' age, which is fair. I do not want to date someone whose mother is my age.

TESSA

You have to have things in common with them. A guy Luc's age probably doesn't have much in common with women our age.

JADE

Surely you have something in common?

TESSA

He works three service jobs and I'm saving for retirement!

I can't relate to working three jobs. I've never even had two.

JADE

Hence why he's a great weekend fling prospect.

I laugh, alone at my table in Paris, and remind myself that even if I don't have a fiancé—fake or real—at least, I have these ladies.

6

Tessa

I WAKE UP OVERHEATED. THE AIR CONDITIONING IN MY HOTEL room cranks out cool air, but I'm flushed all over. Hot flash? No. A dream. It takes a moment for me to remember what I was dreaming about—Luc.

I kick off the covers and stretch my legs in the dim morning light. When I got back to the hotel last night, slightly tipsy from the hefty last glass of wine, I showered off the day —the sweat of walking all over Paris in the summer but also the echoes of Luc's touch on my skin—and changed into a tank top and sleep shorts. I tidied up my things to make room for my friend's stuff and sunk into bed, exhausted.

Now I kick off the shorts, leaving just my underwear. In my dream, Luc had me by the back of the neck again, just like he'd held me in front of James. Unlike in real life, though, I was bent over Luc's body on the bed, his fingers digging into my flesh as he guided my mouth over his cock.

I touch myself, my hand sliding over the curve of my breasts and the swell of my stomach to between my legs. My

43

panties are damp from arousal, and my clit swells under my fingers.

What would Luc feel like? Taste like? I close my eyes and return to my fantasy. In my mind, he's watching me, gazing down on me with that flirtatious twinkle in his eye and dirty words on his lips.

My frustration is building, and my foot is stuck under the covers, so I sit up, strip off my panties, and shove the fluffy duvet hard enough that it tumbles off the foot of the bed. I lay back and close my eyes and pull up the image of Luc looking down at me again. His fingers tighten on the back of my neck, he leaks pre-cum into my mouth, his muscles under my hands strain with desire. It's erotic, and it has me using both hands, spreading myself and using two fingers to circle my clit. I arch off the bed, my legs tensing and straining along with Imaginary Luc, and I'm just about—

"AH!"

The scream at the door jolts me upright, and I'm confronted with the sight of my three best friends scrambling to try to get out of the doorway. Jade, who was likely leading the charge, is trying to exit and close the door, but Emma stands in her way, her hands over her eyes.

"Emma, move!" Jade cries while averting her eyes. I scramble for the covers, but I've kicked them so far, they are on the floor. I manage to grab one edge, but it's caught under the corner of the mattress so that when I pull, the bed underneath me shifts instead of the sheet.

"Sorry, Tessa!" Emma calls and steps back, but she trips over the luggage behind her. In Jade's haste to close the door, she closes it too quickly, and it bounces off her heel and wide open, hitting the door stop.

Jade goes down with a cry, and Emma makes a noise like the wind's knocked out of her.

Finally, the sheet gives, and I'm able to wrap it around myself.

All the while, I can hear Sara cackling down the hall.

"I'm covered!" My cheeks are hot.

"I'm sorry!" Jade returns. "We were trying to sneak in. We thought you were still asleep since you didn't answer your phone."

"It's okay. I'm sorry too. I don't even know what time it is." I reach for my phone and check the time. Seven thirteen.

When I look back, my friends are huddled in the doorway. Sara has calmed her laughter down, although she's struggling not to giggle, and Emma's face is bright red.

Jade just grins at me. Then her eyes widen. "Wait, is Luc here?"

"No, he's not. For Pete's sake, come in. Let me put pants on." I sweep my panties and shorts off the floor and bring them into the bathroom with me and my undignified toga.

When I come out fully dressed, there are hugs all around and more apologies for surprising me.

"I can't believe I didn't pee my pants laughing," Sara says. "It was close."

"We know now never to surprise Tessa." Jade cackles again.

"Can we just pretend it didn't happen?" Emma asks, second-hand embarrassment making her cheeks just as red as mine.

Jade hooks her arm around my shoulders. "We're lucky Tessa was alone and not with *Luc.*" She sing-songs his name.

"All right all right." I elbow Jade, and she laughs.

There have been times that we've seen each other's bodies —I've seen Sara's breasts when she had a cancer scare, and Jade has mooned me more times than I can count—but never quite like this. The teasing will, I'm sure, continue throughout the weekend.

This morning has already been a flurry of emotions—horniness, pleasure, and mortification—but I am also buzzing in excitement because I get to see these wonderful women again.

Despite the early morning travel and unexpected eyeful, the ladies all look happy and chipper as they quickly settle their suitcases and bathroom stuff and tell me about their trips.

Jade's a high-energy person who loves to travel. She's dressed comfortably and has pulled back her thick, long, dark brown hair with a gray streak in her usual ponytail. She packed a small backpack, which she throws on the couch before checking out our view.

Sara, the yoga instructor, with leggings and a loose tank top on her fit body and her brown hair pulled up in a loose bun, is a real-life catalog for athleisure stores. Her small duffle bag sits on the bed—not the one I slept in—and she pulls out some tea and agave nectar and puts them next to the coffee machine.

The biggest suitcase is Emma's. She's never traveled outside the US before, so this is all pretty new. She unpacks, putting her clothes into the drawers.

My stomach rumbles. "Have y'all eaten yet?"

Emma, who still can't look me in the eye, responds first. "I'm starving."

The other two agree, and after I've changed clothes, we head downstairs to the restaurant in the hotel.

All of my good vibes crash when we exit the elevator and I catch sight of James walking across the marble floor of the lobby. In all the excitement of the morning, I'd forgotten that he was here, and I can't duck out because he's already spotted us.

"Well, if it isn't the famous wine club." He's wearing workout clothes, athletic shorts and a T-shirt, which makes me want to scoff.

"James," Jade says stiffly. "Where's your new fiancée?"

"She's having brunch with her parents. Where's *your* fiancé?" James directs the question at me.

"He's sleeping."

"Sure. Of course. Long night being a tour guide?"

I give James a sharp look. "Don't be a dick."

He raises his hands in innocence. "That wasn't my intention."

Jade mutters something that sounds an awful lot like "twatwaffle".

"And as my *friends*," James continues, "maybe you'd like to come to the party tonight celebrating our engagement. I flew Yumi's parents and her friends in, of course. You won't know anyone, but you can bring your *fiancé*. It's at Siempre."

Of course, it's at Siempre, James' favorite club. It's also trendy, and Jade's head snaps up at the mention of it.

"I'll have to see if Luc is free," I hedge.

"I'll text you the details and put you on the list," he says. "Just in case."

He walks toward the elevators with a wave. The four of us resume walking to the restaurant and get to our table in relative quiet.

Once we're in our seats, I put my head in my hands. "Oh my god. We have to go to the party, don't we?"

"Of course not!" Sara frowns at me. "Why would we go?"

"What would James think if we didn't go?"

"Look," Jade says. "You know I'd love to go back to Siempre. But I don't give a fuck about what James thinks, and neither should you."

The table's quiet for a moment.

"Is Siempre the club with the silk dancers and the five-story dance floor? The one you went to after that cancer research seminar?" Sara asks.

"It is," Jade confirms.

"Damn. That place sounded pretty cool."

"The place is huge," I admit. "We probably wouldn't have

to even talk to James if we didn't want to. And I bet he has a VIP room booked."

"He only invited you to rub it in your face," Emma points out.

"I know," I say. "But it's one of the best nightclubs in a city that's very good at nightclubs." Siempre is always in the social pages with rock stars and socialites. Anyone who's throwing a party at Siempre is wealthy—and showing off.

So typical of James.

"Can we also take a minute to acknowledge that James obviously planned an engagement party before proposing?" Emma says. "How uncouth."

"He's an asshat," Jade agrees.

"All the more reason for us not to go," Sara says, pulling the discussion back on track.

You can bring your fiancé, James said. The opportunity to see Luc again intrigues me. If he's available.

"I could see if Luc is available tonight. He might be working."

Jade looks skeptical. "Are you sure?"

"Yeah, I am." Feeling more confident now, I sit up. "It would be fun for us to go clubbing together. We've never done that before and what better place to do it? Sara, Zoe would absolutely die to know her mother's been clubbing at Siempre. And Jade, you've said so yourself; you love the place. How about this: if Luc can come, we'll take it as a sign to go. If not, then we'll skip it."

Jade smirks. "If we're gonna go, then you'll definitely need to have your young, hot fiancé on your arm to shove in James' face."

I text Luc, and we get on with our brunch. He doesn't answer right away, but I check my phone as we're leaving the hotel, and there's a message from him.

LUC

I am free tonight. Send me the details and I'll
meet you at your hotel.

Jade and Sara are absolutely ecstatic to be going to Siempre. Even Emma warms up to the idea, though she was never
one to be into bars or clubbing. Like Sara, she married young
and had kids quickly, so there was never time for her to be a
rebellious youth. But unlike widowed Sara, Emma's marriage
lasted decades and ended in divorce. Nerves and anxiety
temper newly single Emma's excitement.

My phone pings with another message from Luc.

LUC

Take your friends via the Pont des Arts. On a
day like today, it'll be brimming with artists
and buskers.

I read it and adjust course, guiding the group to the pedes-
trian bridge.

I tell myself that the excited butterflies in my stomach are
about having a fun night out and not about the possibility of
seeing Luc again.

Liar.

7

Luc

Tessa was on my mind all day while I worked the lunch shift at the bar. When I woke up this morning and had a message from her inviting me out tonight, I was thrilled at the chance to see her again and to go to Siempre. I've had friends who've worked there, and the stories about the clientele are outrageous.

No one should miss a chance to go to Siempre, and it would be a memorable time for them. I also think about Tessa showing up alone and James and Yumi thinking that, at worst, I'm not really her fiancé, or at best, the truth—I'm too busy working three jobs and am completely out of my league with Tessa.

So, I tell her I can go. What I really mean is I'll work my shift at the bar and cancel driving for the night. Yeah, it's a sizeable chunk out of my pay for the week to not drive on a Saturday night, but I will do it for Tessa.

I want to know her better, and I want to meet her friends.

As I'm closing my tabs and checking out, my phone pings.

I smile. I've been sending Tessa tips for her friends, trying to make up for them not having a tour guide. She's been texting back, thanking me and sending pictures of them having fun around the city.

The streets are busy as I walk home in the early evening, and if I was driving, I'd make a ton of money.

Not for the first time, I lament that I have to work three jobs. But a year ago, when Mémé brought up the idea of retiring, I encouraged her to do it. She always worked retail jobs, which were hard on her mentally. She took care of me growing up, so it was my turn to take care of her. All the money I can spare goes to my grandmother, and I just thank god that she owns her apartment.

Thinking of Mémé, the cash from tips in my pocket, and the party tonight, I detour over to her place. I have time before I meet Tessa and her friends. They complained about starting late, but I assured them that if we showed up when they wanted, the party wouldn't have even started yet.

When Mémé opens the door and spots me with the takeaway I picked up on my way over, she reprimands me for the thousandth time. "You don't have to knock, Luc. You have a key. Use it," she grumbles.

"I never know what you are up to in here. Don't want to walk in on anything indecent."

I mean a gentleman caller, like the kind I walked in on a few months ago, but Mémé snorts. "Soon, you'll be taking care of me, changing my diapers and spoon-feeding me. Get used to seeing it now."

I roll my eyes. Mémé is nowhere near needing that level of care. She should be dating, not worrying about me caring for her when she needs it—if she needs it. Mémé, like most

French women her age, smokes and drinks and walks all over the city and is svelte and energetic. Since retiring, she's much happier, and I'm proud to provide for her now.

"Wine?" she asks me as she heads to the kitchen.

"Please," I say. While she's occupied, I pull my tips out of my pocket and slide the bills under a book on the coffee table. She might not find it for a while, but if she's caught on that I'm leaving extra money around for her, she's never said.

"Shouldn't you be driving tonight?" she calls. I walk into the kitchen, my heart aching when I see the Styrofoam containers on the counter. For as long as I've remembered, Mémé has found every way that she can to pinch pennies, including washing and reusing disposable containers and never wasting food.

It's not that those things are inherently bad, but she takes it too far. One cabinet overflows with these containers. Sometimes I clean out her fridge for her because I worry about her health. I've seen her more than once cut mold off of food and eat what remains, and at her age, she shouldn't be taking that risk.

"No, I'm going to a friend's party tonight," I say, addressing her question about my evening plans.

"A girl's?" she asks.

I kiss her cheek as she hands me a glass of cold white wine. "An engagement party at Siempre. But with a woman, yes."

Mémé's eyebrows raise. "Siempre? Fancy."

"She is."

Mémé, with her impeccably clean Dior outfit, one that she's owned for at least a decade but bought at a second-hand shop, looks me over. "What are you going to wear?"

I grimace, but before I can even say anything, she's picked up her phone.

"Bernice, darling, do you have some time?"

8

Tessa

After a second day in a row of walking around Paris, this one complete with two museums, catching up with my friends, and laying in the sun, we have to take a nap. Thank goodness European parties start late.

When the alarm goes off, Jade rolls over and whacks me in the face, trying to shut it off. We're sharing the bed I rumpled thinking about Luc, though the sheets are clean now. I turn off the alarm, take Jade's pillow, and throw it at the other bed.

"Time to get up, bitches," Jade says through a yawn.

We turn on music, order a bottle of wine from room service, and start throwing around clothes. Jade arrived in Paris with only a small carry-on bag while Sara and Emma over-packed. But I shouldn't have underestimated Jade; from her tiny carry-on, she pulls out skinny cropped pants, a shimmery tank top, and strappy heels.

This afternoon, after touring the city and a very late and long Parisian lunch, we went shopping. Since Sara's wardrobe is ninety-five percent yoga pants and Emma leans toward mom jeans and flowy floral dresses, we needed to get them something to wear for the night.

My outfit is a black bandage dress. I squeeze into it and admire the cut in the mirror, smoothing my hands down the wide-hip-and-soft-belly hugging material. At forty-two and a lot of therapy, I've learned to love my body, despite what the world—or even my mother—tells me. She used to call me "pear-shaped" and insisted I got it from my dad's side of the family. Looking at myself now, in this sexy dress with my best friends and a very hot fiancé—even if he is fake—I give the rest of the world a big fucking middle finger.

Jade's the first one ready, her hair up in her signature high ponytail, the streak of gray a stark contrast to her thick, dark hair. She wears a pair of skinny cropped pants and a shimmery top hugging her slim frame. Her eyes are smoky and dark, accentuating her bronze skin, and she turns her attention to convincing Sara to let her do her makeup. Sara rarely wears makeup, but finally gives in.

"Tessa, do you think Veronica will be there?" Jade asks. Sara sits in front of her, eyes closed, while Jade applies eye shadow. I'm twisting Sara's long dark hair into a bun at the nape of her neck to combat the Parisian summer air and the heat of the club later.

I frown. James's mom doesn't like to travel, and she wasn't there yesterday. "I don't know. I haven't spoken to her in months." I didn't just lose James with the breakup; I lost his mom, too. With my own mother's declining mental faculties, Veronica and I had gotten close.

Emma emerges from the bathroom in the dress she bought this afternoon. It's a bright red faux wrap, which flatters Emma's height and build. There's a wide matching belt that accentuates her waist, and it is very low cut, so I picked out a black lace cami to go underneath.

We wolf-whistle at her until she blushes and smacks my shoulder with the back of her hand playfully. I give her a fishtail braid, her mostly gray hair draping over one shoulder and teasing the top of her breasts.

I remember the night at the wine bar two years ago when Emma decided to stop dying her hair. While Jade has always been proud of her gray streak, which fits her so well, Sara was just starting to obsess about the scattered gray hairs that were coming into her dark brown hair, and she'd asked Emma for dying tips. A few at-home hair dye experiences later, they resolved to let their hair be natural.

My blonde is light enough that you can't see the grays much, especially when I have my hair smoothed back like it is now. Emma thinks that's why I look like the youngest of the group, but I've always admired her salt-and-pepper hair now that she stopped dyeing it.

"We should do this every month when we get together," Jade says. "A girl's night out. Really dress up and go out on the town."

Sara checks herself out in the full-length mirror and brightens up. She reaches for her phone and snaps a picture. "Zoe is going to die when she sees me like this. Maybe she can join us when you come to Baden-Baden."

Emma looks less sure, but that might be more about the dress than money worries. I catch Jade's eye, and she glances at Emma, staring at herself in the mirror.

Jade slides her arm around Emma's waist. "You look fucking bangable in that dress, I promise. We'll be fending men off all night. But if it makes you uncomfortable, don't wear it, okay? We can come up with something else."

Emma tilts her chin up. "I like it, I swear. It's just . . ." Jade releases Emma. "I don't think I've ever felt this sexy in my life."

"Get used to it, babe. Now, Tessa," Jade says while sidling over to me, "you've been in a very good mood today. Would that have anything to do with the fiancé?" She bats her eyelashes at me.

Fortunately, I'm saved from answering because Luc texts that he's downstairs, so I herd my friends out the door. He's waiting in the lobby, sitting in one of the large upholstered chairs when we get out of the elevator.

He's in slim charcoal pants and a fitted button-up shirt, and he styled his hair. It still has a bit of that wild, tousled look, but somewhat caged.

Jade looks him over and nods approvingly.

He doesn't notice, though. His gaze is on me, and I feel his eyes run up from my heels to the top of my head. My blonde hair is up in a twist, my face contoured, and the dress hides nothing. The Hervé Léger fits me like a glove, and Luc's eyes heat up as he takes me in.

Jade hisses and waves her hand like she's fanning away smoke. "Please, don't mind us. Just eye fuck each other."

That snaps me out of it. "Hush, you. Luc, you look great."

"So do you," he says, and touches a hand to my waist. He winks and leans in. "You look fucking amazing."

A throat clears, and Luc humors Jade. "You all do," he corrects himself. I make introductions, and Luc shakes hands with each of them. Then he slides his arm around my waist.

"Oh," I say quickly. "You don't have to pretend to be my fiancé around them."

Luc squeezes me closer, but before he can respond, Jade interrupts. "Please, it's such a hardship for him to put his hands on you."

"Also," Luc says, reaching into his pocket. He pulls something out and uncurls his fist, revealing a diamond ring. It's simple, princess-cut and maybe a carat in size.

"Oh, Luc," I whisper. "You don't have to do this."

"Try it on," he suggests and then breaks our embrace. His hand trails down my left arm, gathering my hand in his, and I spread my fingers.

The ring slips on perfectly, Luc's hands sure as if he knew it would, and emotions well inside me. No one has ever put a ring on my finger. A part of me whispers that it isn't real, but a bigger part gazes at the beautiful, simple ring and wonders what the harm is in feeling loved and cherished for a night.

I swallow and clear my throat. "Is this your grandmother's?"

"It is. I told her about you, and she loves a good revenge story." His arms wrap me in a hug. His voice is rough when he says, "It looks good on you."

I stare at the ring for a few more seconds after he lets me go and then glance up. My friends are all watching us, a mixture of amusement and swooning.

I brush it off and straighten, lightening the mood. "Are we ready to go dance like no one's watching in front of hundreds of people?"

My friends laugh, and as we move, Jade takes Luc's arm. They lead us out the doors, held by the hotel staff, and toward the metro.

Sara and Emma walk on either side of me. "He is really cute," Sara says, leaning close to me.

"I know."

"Like, *really* cute," Emma adds.

As if he knows we're talking about him, Luc glances back at us and winks at me.

My three friends are chatty and loud, Jade peppering Luc with questions before finally releasing him to talk with us, trying to set some ground rules for if anyone wants to hook up with a man tonight. By unspoken agreement, Luc and I let them get ahead of us while they debate locations. His hand catches mine while we walk.

"Maybe we should have an origin story, you know? How did we meet?"

"True. Okay, when would we have met . . ." I tap my chin with my free hand. "Have you ever been to Houston? That's where I grew up."

"No, I've never been to the States. But you've been here a lot, so maybe we should just say we met here."

I wrinkle my nose. "Well, the last time was with James, about a year ago."

"What if we met online?"

"Like a dating app?"

"Or through friends?"

I pull my phone out of my purse and click open Facebook. "Let's see if we have any friends in common."

Luc opens his, too, and we find—and friend—each other. "No friends in common." Luc frowns at his phone, and I can see he's scrolling through my profile.

"It's weird to see you Facebook stalking me in person."

He flashes a grin. "What about Instagram?"

Same thing. No friends in common. We clack down the stairs to the metro, where Sara, Jade, and Emma are waiting with their phones out. "Luc, what's your last name?" Jade asks.

He tells them, and they each bury themselves in social media trying to track down a common thread as we wait for the metro.

"Ah ha!" Jade says. "We have a friend in common, Luc!"

"We do?" His eyebrow raises, and he peers over Jade's shoulder.

"Six degrees of separation can suck it. In today's technology, it's more like two," Jade crows. "I bet I could find a connection to anyone. Two degrees to Harry Styles. Or Verduistering!" Her eyes light up, devious.

"Who's . . . Verdas . . .?" Sara asks.

"Verduistering. They're a band. They won Eurovision last year." At Sara's confused face, Jade continues. "It's a huge music competition with acts from all over Europe. You should watch it," she says as we board the subway and take our seats.

"Okay," I interrupt before we get too off track. "How do you know Luc's friend?"

Jade shows Luc the picture of a young woman who looks like she's on a sailboat, drinking a beer and wearing enormous sunglasses.

"Oh, Elayna? We went to school together."

"University?" I ask.

"I didn't go to university," Luc says with a shake of his head. "Primary school. When did you meet her?" he asks Jade.

"In the Caribbean. She was tutoring French and working in a bakery at a resort I went to."

"Wow, that is a tenuous connection," Sara says, rightfully doubtful.

But Jade shrugs the doubt away. "Honestly, no one's going to want details. Just say you two were friends of friends, and Luc slid into your DMs one day. Or," she says, and I can see the wheels spinning. "What if I played matchmaker online? You met the love of your life because I told you to check out the hottie on Insta?" She's scrolling on her phone, head tilting. "Luc, seriously, no shirtless pics that I can point to and say, 'Tessa, check out this hottie?'"

I snatch Jade's phone away from her, and she rolls her eyes.

"I followed him. I'll just check it out later."

"Umm . . . we all just followed him," Sara says. "Is it going to be weird that we all just followed your fiancé at once?"

I look down at my phone. I suppose I should click the button to follow him too, because shouldn't I be following my fiancé on Insta?

We're all quiet for a moment. "Ugh," Sara breaks the silence. "Friending people in a digital age is weird."

"Agree," Jade says.

"Also, can we all agree that our engagement being fake stays between the five of us?" I ask. This is embarrassing enough already, but I know that once this night is over, I won't ever see James, his fiancée, or anyone else at this stupid party again.

Sara grimaces. "I already told Zoe."

"Okay, the six of us, then."

There's a chorus of yeses and head nods.

Luc's been quiet, scrolling on his phone, and sitting next to him like this, I can see he's going through my Facebook feed. Fun pictures with my friends, often posted by one of their kids tagging me, but also dinners with my family, my sister's wedding, and lunches with my sorority sisters.

I look around the metro car, and we're all in our phones, dressed up for clubbing. "Hey," I snap my fingers. "We're going out clubbing at Siempre, not hiding in our phones."

"Yes!" Sara is on board, sitting up and putting her phone back into her clutch. "I am so excited, my first club!"

Luc laughs, bewildered. "Really?"

Sara bats her eyelashes. "In college, I was dating Kit—my late husband. We got married right after graduation, and Zoe came along the next year. There was no time for clubbing." That's true, but it's also true that Sara's been single for over fifteen years. Instead of trying to find a partner again, she focused all her attention on raising Zoe.

"Well, I definitely could use a fun night out and release some tension." Jade shakes her head. "With moving and getting settled into my new apartment and office in Madrid, I haven't had time to socialize."

Sara and I exchange glances. Jade's talked a lot about a guy in her office, Carlos, and we're pretty sure she has a crush on the Clark-Kent lookalike. He was attractive, single, and best of all, not in her department, but he turned her down when she asked him out.

The metro lurches to a halt, and it's our stop. When we step out, Jade hooks her arm through Luc's. "You know, I should have asked if you have any cute, single friends who could have come tonight."

We laugh and pile out of the station. It's only a few blocks before we stand at the entrance of Siempre, and I brace myself to see James again.

9

Luc

WE PASS THROUGH THE BOUNCER—OUR NAME IS ON THE LIST FOR James' party, and he gives us wristbands—and follow a hostess to one of the VIP rooms, passing beneath enormous chandeliers. A dancer hangs from the largest one, hanging from her feet, which are tangled in a black silk ribbon. Gilded mirrors line the walls and make the space seem enormous. It's very Versailles-meets-sex-dungeon.

The VIP room is not as packed with people as the main floors. We get served drinks immediately, and I am thrilled to learn it is paid for. They must be spending a fortune on this party.

Drinks in hand, we wade through to the glassed balcony overlooking the main dance floor. Emma's next to me, and her mouth makes a perfect O as she gazes down at the masses. House music floods the giant room, the pulse vibrating down to my chest. Tessa curls her arm around my waist, and I return the side embrace with my arm around her shoulder.

To everyone in this room, we're a couple, and the thought sends a flutter up my chest.

After the initial excitement wears off, we meet a few people around us, small talk presides, and no one asks Tessa and me how we met.

Jade disappears as we all talk about the music, the party, the people.

I feel like a wolf in sheep's clothing. I had already suspected that Tessa was out of my league, but watching her, dressed up like she belongs here, happily chatting with her friends at one of the hottest clubs in Paris like it's nothing doesn't sit well with me.

Her photos on Facebook didn't help, either. Her family looks rich and wholesome, and Tessa a carbon copy of her mother, who looks refined like my grandmother, but in a colder way. There are pictures at galas and charity events, Tessa raising money for those less fortunate.

I am glad Mémé called in a favor. Bernice owns the second-hand shop down the street and, at my grandmother's request, met us there and opened her doors after hours for us. It's high-end clothes, and though Mémé combs through it every week, she rarely buys anything. Bernice calls her when something she might like comes in.

The clothes I'm wearing now make me fit right in. Bernice assured me I can clean them and return them to her, which means it didn't cost me anything.

I'm jarred out of my thoughts by Jade's return. She holds a tray of shots, neon green. I'm thankful for something to do.

"Can we go downstairs to dance?" Jade asks. She's been swaying and moving ever since we got here, and she gazes hopefully at Tessa.

But it's Sara who answers. "Two shots, finish your drink, and then yes!"

We each grab the tiny plastic shot glasses and raise them

in a toast. I don't know what I'm drinking, but it's potent and sickly sweet as it slides down my throat.

Tessa turns down the next shot, and Emma just shrugs and takes it instead, hammering down two in a row, a move that surprises her friends. Jade washes down the shot with her gin and tonic, holding up the empty glass when she's done.

We move down to the dancefloor, Tessa's fingers twined with mine. When there's room, I twirl her, and she laughs, though I can barely hear it over the music. Gracefully, she spins toward me, her back to my front, and my hands go to her hips.

With Tessa's head on my shoulder, her ass fitting into me perfectly, I am barely aware of anything around us. I let my nose run up the shell of her ear, my eyes half-closed while I breathe her in. Her ass is giving me ideas. Lots of them. Ideas that make me think about this beautiful, poised woman getting filthy with me.

I wasn't expecting a second night with Tessa, never mind getting to see her dressed up, so sexy and beautiful while she dances. I want to strip her down, spend some time with Tessa's body, uninterrupted time where I can make her limp and satisfied.

This dancing, though, is torture. I'm hard for at least a dozen songs. We're both sweaty, and I just want to get Tessa alone.

We weave our way off of the dance floor and up the stairs. It's blissfully quieter in the stairwell, and I tug on Tessa's hand. She slows, and we fall back from her friends and linger in the stairwell. "You're quite the dancer."

She laughs. "I love it. I haven't danced in ages. Maybe we'll go back after our water break."

Tessa's leaning against the wall, and with me being a few centimeters taller than her in her heels, she has to look up to meet my eyes. We're quiet for a few moments, tucked into this corner of the landing. I can hear the music pumping from below, laughter and conversation from the room half a floor below us.

All of that fades away as I step closer, placing my hand on Tessa's hip, smoothing my fingers over the fabric and warm skin underneath. Her eyes widen, her chin tilting further up, her soft lips just begging for me to taste them.

I do. I meet her parted lips with mine and swallow the small sound of surprise she makes. Her lips are just as soft as I thought they'd be, the mild flavor of cosmetics giving way to sweetness and warmth.

Tessa clutches at me and opens her mouth, pulling me closer and deeper into her. It's just my tongue now, but I want more of me inside of her, thrusting and wet and heavy.

I want to take Tessa home and make her scream.

Voices get louder, and laughter erupts, reminding me that we're in public. One of those voices sounds familiar, too.

When the person comes into view, it's James. I glance back at Tessa.

A possessive wave rolls over me. She's disheveled, her lips swollen from the kiss, and her eyes dazed. I did that to her.

She notices James, her eyes sharpening. I look back in time to see James realize who we are, just as he's about to set foot on the first stair above the landing. He falters for just a moment and then continues, still talking. He's got a good poker face, but I saw a flash of something.

I turn back to Tessa. Her eyes are closed, and I slide my hand to her neck and use my thumb to tilt her chin up so I can take her mouth again. My first thought is that I hope he turns around and sees us, but that fades away because all that really matters is that I'm kissing Tessa. This time it's sweeping and stroking, long kisses that light me up, and I barely notice as the voices fade into the party upstairs.

But they do, and I break away from her, grinning and

pleased with myself. "Come on," I say, stepping away and offering her my hand. "Let's go catch up to your friends."

We find Emma and Sara seated on a couch, a low table in front of them. Tessa sits in one of the upholstered chairs across from them, and I perch on the arm of the chair. "Jade went to get water," Sara explains, and in a few moments, Jade is there passing out water bottles. She's frowning, and after a few sips, she speaks. "I bumped into Yumi at the bar. I don't think she knew who I was."

Tessa grimaces. "How did that go?"

Jade's eyes flick to the side once, and Tessa's mouth tilts into a frown. Jade squares her shoulders and sets her jaw. "We got to talking and . . . Tessa, they've been dating for eight months."

Emma gasps, and Tessa falls slack against the chair. I remember our conversation yesterday where Tessa said they'd broken up five months ago. I put a hand on her shoulder, wanting to comfort her. All she wanted was a fun weekend with her friends, and it's been hit after hit. I want nothing more than to wipe it all away for her. Jade notices my touch and gives me a small smile of gratitude.

"He was cheating on me?"

Jade paces the small space in front of the couch, and Sara and Emma touch Tessa, comforting hands surrounding her.

"There's more." Jade's voice is tight and strained. "I don't think she knew you two were still dating. She made some comment, and I couldn't quite catch it over the music, but it was something about James and . . ." She shakes her head. "Sorry, I should have asked her to repeat it, but I just wanted to get the hell away from her."

There's a moment of quiet where all I can hear is the beat of the music, and Jade and Sara's awkward glances at me are nearly audible even over that noise.

Until something behind me catches Sara's eye. "Oh shit, they're coming here. Someone, I don't know, laugh?"

Emma busts out a cackle, and it's so loud and unexpected that it even makes Tessa crack a smile—a wobbly one, but still.

"Girls, looking lovely this evening. Tessa." James nods at her, a smarmy smile in place. *Cheater*, a nasty voice in my head says. "And . . . Luc, was it?" At my glare, he ignores me and turns to introduce Emma, Sara, and Jade to his fiancée.

"We've met," Jade says, baring her teeth in a smile that's more threatening than friendly, and Yumi's own smile fades, her eyebrows knitting together in confusion over Jade's bitter tone.

"Tessa," James starts, and I feel a warning in my gut that Tessa's going to be hurt once more before he leaves us. "I called my mom last night and mentioned that I saw you here. She was surprised to hear that you were engaged now."

He rolls the ice in his glass as he gestures at me. "She called your mom, and imagine our surprise when your mom didn't know a thing about Luc, either. I would think your mom would know about your fiancé. Hell, I'm sure my mother would remember you even mentioning that you were dating someone, but she doesn't. Funny, that."

Tessa's entire focus is on her ex-boyfriend, her confusion and disbelief from before morphed into something that's sharpened and honed.

James chuckles, totally unaware of how big of a moron he is.

Tessa rises to her feet. Emma and Sara pop up next to her, and Jade folds her arms and glowers at James.

"As much as I love your mother, James, surely you wouldn't expect me to tell her I've moved on to someone else. She knows that we've broken up. I bet she even remembers the date we broke up," Tessa seethes.

Jade grins, and I chuckle under my breath, but Tessa's not done.

"She probably remembers the date we broke up, *and* I bet

she remembers the last time I stayed the night at your parent's house, and we shared their bedroom. I bet she remembers hinting to you to propose soon so that there was still time to get the announcement in the Chronicle before the flood of Valentine's Day proposals filled it up."

James' mouth flops a bit, and for a moment, I feel bad for Yumi because she's gone pale. While Tessa *wanted* to be James' fiancée, Yumi is, and she's just been told that she was the other woman.

Emma hooks her arm through Tessa's and says stiffly, "Thank you for the invitation."

Sara hooks Tessa's other side. "Don't invite us to the wedding."

"You deserve better," Jade shouts over her shoulder to Yumi as we head for the door.

10

Tessa

ONCE WE'RE OUT ON THE STREET, JADE AND SARA BURST INTO laughter, giddy from insulting James. Emma grips my arm tightly, not quite ready to relax and give up her concern, and I glance back over my shoulder at Luc. He's got his hands in his pockets, watching Jade and Sara with amusement.

I like that he didn't take control of the situation. He was supportive, but in the battle of the wit between James and me, Luc let me lead. I've had plenty of men try to do my fighting for me as if I can't stand up for myself.

He agreed to be my fake fiancé tonight. I could have given an excuse for why he couldn't come or confessed that it was a joke. Instead, I'm breaking up an engagement and faking my own, on top of making out with him in front of my ex.

Walking into Siempre earlier had felt like visiting my old high school. It's familiar, the same walls, the same sounds as last time I was here, but everyone looks like babies. Even in the VIP room, everyone was younger than us. I would have placed Yumi as in her late thirties, but that may have been in the context of seeing her with James. Now, around youthful friends and party-goers, I realize she might be younger than I thought.

Not that I have room to judge since the man I'm currently "engaged" to and just made out with is in his early thirties.

But the loud music, young faces, and the heat of the party was wearing on me. I was the one who wanted to come to this party, and now I've fought with James and made a public scene.

This has become a giant mess. I've never acted so immature in my life.

The thought angers me.

"What was I thinking?" I ask. Jade and Sara straighten and finally get their laughter under control.

"You're thinking he's a cheating cheater who deserves it." Jade reaches out and grabs my hand. "Don't feel bad for James. He made his own bed, and now he can lie in it."

"I don't feel bad for him. But what the hell am I doing? I'm in a *fake engagement* with Luc." I throw my hand out to gesture at him. "And having petty, small-minded feelings about my ex. I'm a forty-two-year-old woman, for fuck's sake. Life isn't supposed to be this complicated or embarrassing by now."

Our group is silent, and I realize how that must have sounded. If I hadn't been drinking, if I hadn't been frustrated with myself and angry at James, maybe I wouldn't have said it, but I did. "Luc, not you. I didn't mean you."

He laughs, but it's got no humor in it. "I know that I am aiming out of my league here, Tessa."

"I don't . . . I'm not out of your league," I say with vehemence. "Regardless, I didn't mean it. You aren't embarrassing me. It's just my behavior." I feel like an idiot, and Luc's probably glad I'm only here for a weekend.

With that thought, I remember that it's my last night in Paris, and my stupid mouth, usually controlled and well-behaved, ruined it.

Luc's mouth tightens for a moment, and Emma, Jade, and Sara take a few steps away to give us privacy.

"I am so sorry I dragged you into all this and said those things. You've been so kind to me this weekend, and that's no way to treat a friend—especially not a fake fiancé." He watches me for a few heartbeats before the lines around his mouth ease. I like those lines a lot better when it's his infectious smile causing them.

I reach for his hand, and he gives me it. "I'm sorry."

Luc tugs hard enough that I fall forward, a hand on his chest as he catches me. "Thank you," he says in French. His voice is low and in my ear, causing a shiver to roll up my spine. "For what it's worth, you handled the situation with grace. You didn't make a scene; you didn't confront him. He did it to himself. You were much more mature than most people would have been in that situation."

I smile at the compliment and drop his hand. I press both my palms to his chest between us and look up at him. We may have been faking our relationship and kissing for show, but I know that I'll kick myself if I don't take a chance to enjoy myself with this kind, flirty man.

Dancing with Luc was so fun. So many guys I've dated are uptight about dancing. James was like that, unable to get his hips to relax and feel the music. But Luc slipped right in, and we quickly found a rhythm together, bodies moving with the beat, his hand on my waist, pressing his whole body and grinding against me while protectively surrounding me.

Luc is not my typical kind of guy. But his flirting and his dancing have me wondering what it would be like to go back to his place and have a wild, out-of-character night before I fly to Portugal and am out of his life.

I've never dated someone much younger than me, and I can't help but think about how women peak sexually later in life. Is it possible to have the best sex of your life in your forties? The thought makes me shiver.

Perhaps this is an opportunity for me to find out.

I gaze up at Luc. "I want to invite you home with me tonight. However, I do have three roommates." I dramatically glance over at my friends, all of whom quickly glance away, and Luc's chuckle reverberates in his chest.

He looks down at me with a lopsided smile full of affection, which makes my heart swell. All forgiven.

But then he sighs and rakes a hand through his hair, the death blow to his styled hair that's made it through a sweaty dance floor, and I wonder if I'm not so easily forgiven.

"My flat is . . ." He cringes. "Not very nice."

"Oh, Luc," I say, pulling him against me. "I want to be with you. I promise you; your place doesn't matter. Maybe this is a good lesson for us to learn," I say, tilting my head toward my friends. "If *someone*,"—I cough with faux-discretion — "Jade,"—cough, cough. Luc laughs—"were to bring a man home, then perhaps we should book two hotel rooms for our weekend getaways."

"Connected rooms!" Jade shouts, proving they've been eavesdropping.

"All right," Luc says, and he smiles down at me.

I raise my voice, and the ladies wander back toward us. "I'm going with Luc."

"We're going to head back to the hotel," Sara says. My friends take turns hugging me.

"You know how to get back?" Luc asks.

Jade pats his cheek. "Yes. Give her a good time." She winks before sauntering in the direction of the metro station.

Sara yawns and kisses my cheek. "Proud of you tonight," she whispers in my ear. "I like the boost of confidence you had tonight. I wonder where that came from." She looks pointedly at Luc and smirks at me.

Emma looks pointedly at Luc. "Where do you live?"

Luc rattles off his address, and Emma types it into her

phone. She points two fingers at her eyes and then at his. "Consider this your warning."

Luc just nods, and we wave goodbye to them. "What exactly was Emma's warning?" He pulls out his phone and orders a rideshare while I press my body up against his. "She's threatening to lie in bed worrying about me, call the cops in the morning if she hasn't heard from me by nine, and then she'd unleash Jade on you."

Luc shivers, but I'm pretty sure it's because I've pressed my lips to the hollow of his throat and not because he's worried about Emma's threats. I follow the kiss with a lick. He's salty and musky, and I'm sure we both would appreciate a shower before we tumble into bed.

"Two minutes for our car," he says, putting his phone back in his pocket. "What can we do for two minutes?"

Without hesitation, Luc pulls me to him, and his mouth is on mine again. I nearly stumble in his eagerness, and his lips pressed against mine twist in amusement while he firms his grip. I don't have time to think about the party we've left behind or the kisses in the hallway before I'm drowning in the here and now of kissing a man who's so enthusiastic about going home with me.

11

Luc

I LEAD TESSA QUICKLY THROUGH THE ENTRANCE TO MY apartment building, eager to get her naked and taste her. We'd made out in front of the club until our driver honked and then moved to the backseat.

I guide her into my apartment. My mouth finds hers again as the door snicks shut. Now that we aren't in public, I can't help myself. My hands rove her body, the tight dress and her luscious curves; my kisses wander down, and then I'm on my knees, Tessa's back against the door, her eyes shadowed by the overhead light.

Tessa closes her eyes, and her head lolls back. With my nose this close to the hem of her dress, I can smell her desire. My senses are full of Tessa.

As if she reads my thoughts, Tessa looks down. "Do you want me to shower first?" she asks, breathless, in English now, and I love the idea that I've wiped a whole second language out of her head.

"Can you wait? Can you wait to have my mouth on your cunt and my tongue torturing you?" I ask, my breath skating over her skin and her stomach twitching underneath my hands. I speak in French, wanting to talk to her in my native tongue, too.

She closes her eyes again, and I hear a thunk as her head hits the door. "No," she whispers.

My hands are quick, shoving her hem up to her waist. Her underwear is a simple thong that I can't take my eyes off of while my hands are on autopilot getting her shoes off.

I press my head to her stomach and just breathe in. I slide my palms up both legs, feeling the excitement that tremors just under her skin. My hands stop at her ass, squeezing, and we're both quiet. Tessa's fingers comb through my hair, gently scraping my scalp. Her skin is so smooth and soft, her thighs sloping up and widening to her butt and her plush, round stomach. I love the way my fingers dimple her ass, and I can't wait to do dirty things to it. Whatever Tessa wants, she'll get.

Everything slows down, and I pay attention.

I pay attention to the gasps when I press an open-mouth kiss to the spot of skin in the center of her stomach, just below her belly button and above the band of her panties.

I pay attention when I nuzzle my nose over her hip, and she twitches.

I pay attention when I gently push her knee away from me, opening that joint between her hip and her thigh, and I lick the tendon there. Tessa bucks.

"Luc," she moans.

I stop teasing—mostly—and turn my head, pressing my mouth right into her. Tessa cries out, and I press harder, burying my face into the fabric of her panties. My hands brace, keeping her in place, and I lick her again, this time down her hot core. Underneath my tongue, I feel the folds of her center, the firm clit through the fabric. I gently scrape my teeth over it.

Tessa moans, and I keep at it, licking and playing with her

through the fabric until it's all a mess. She's soaked, and I'm rock hard and straining against my zipper. I moan, letting the vibrations amp her up even more until a hand on my forehead forces me away.

"Bed," Tessa tells me sternly. She squeaks when I pick her up. "Luc, don't. I'm too heavy."

I ignore her concerns and get a knee on the bed before I let go. Tessa bounces gently, and it was a grave error not to get her naked first. I would love to see those tits bounce.

She tugs me down before I can do anything about it, and we're kissing, and my cock rubs against that damp spot my mouth left. It's through three layers of clothing, but I swear I can feel her wetness and heat.

I enjoy thrusting against her, but I don't let it distract me. Resolved to get Tessa naked, I pull back, and together we strip off the dress.

"You too," she says, and I stand and take less than two seconds to get naked while Tessa strips the bed down to the sheets. Then I'm back between her legs and pressing my mouth against her, and she's making ungodly noises and squirming while I suck at her, that perfect little bud that I tease with my lips and tongue and teeth until her thighs clench around me and she shouts my name.

I keep going until she tells me to stop, a hoarse plea. My cock is heavy and tight, and I'm already close. I've been grinding against the bed. No matter what's next, I am not going to last.

Sitting up on my knees, I look down at Tessa spread before me. Her pussy glistens, that flush has bloomed over her chest and up her cheeks, and her belly and chest rise with her panting breaths. She looks glassy and disheveled, and I can't resist taking myself in hand.

Her gaze zeros in on my grip, and I tighten my fist before I reach the point of no return.

"Can I come on you?" I ask, and her eyes light up.

12

Tessa

I STRETCH OUT, MY ARMS OVER MY HEAD, THRUSTING MY BREASTS up. Luc walks his knees up to either side of my hips and strokes himself. It's captivating to watch his lean muscles as he moves, the way his biceps flex as he strokes. The sound is slick and obscene, even knowing that I was just loud as hell myself.

A palm presses into the mattress above my head, and Luc bends over, lips hovering above mine. I can smell myself; Luc's breathing hard, and his mouth, the one that made me come so skillfully, waits for me. I press up and kiss him while he strokes.

Writhing beneath him is the sexiest I have ever felt in my life.

It doesn't take long. His head falls forward, his arm trembles, and I turn my head to kiss the veins that stand out while he strains.

He comes quietly, the opposite of the loud, sloppy mess that I was. In the light cast by the single fixture over the door,

I watch his lean torso and muscles tense and flex while he comes, each drop hitting in a hot flick onto my skin.

With one small grunt, he collapses to the side and releases his cock. The bed dips, and then he kisses my shoulder, a palm coming to my belly and dipping a finger in the mess he made.

"Fuck," he finally says.

I smile at his use of putain. I'm not comfortable enough with my French vocabulary to use it in bed, and I liked our bilingual sex. Hearing Luc use words like le cul and tétons for my ass and boobs was hot.

"Can you stay the night?" he asks, flattening his palm against my skin. "Maybe a shower and then round two?"

"Yes, please."

Luc gets up and retrieves a washcloth from the bathroom, wiping my stomach before we step under the steaming hot shower.

Luc's place is small and run-down, though he keeps it tidy. As small as this shower is, the water is good—high pressure and warm—and I can't keep my hands off of Luc. The suds make everything slick, and I twist my grip around his cock, enjoying the smoothness of his shaft and the grunts he makes when I reach the tip.

Luc pushes me away with a growl. "Bed. Now."

We rinse and dry off in a rush, and I squeak in surprise when Luc pushes me face down onto his bed. He settles between my legs, and I tilt my hips, giving him access to as much of me as he wants. I jolt in surprise when he starts in my center and licks back over my ass. The shock of it is all I can feel at first, but then I get used to it, and Luc's tongue makes me warm and wet and aching.

My legs tighten, and Luc shifts, his arms coming underneath my thighs, and his hands reach back and spread my butt cheeks to give himself more access. I can feel an orgasm building, and he must feel it too, because he focuses on my clit with his tongue.

"Fuck, you taste so good," he says against my skin. When my clit is back in his mouth, I come hard, locking up and letting out a low guttural sound as I come against his face.

As soon as my twitches subside, Luc is up and covering my body. "Can I get a condom? I want to fuck you and watch that ass bounce for me."

"Oh god, yes."

I turn my head so I can watch Luc walk naked back to the bathroom and retrieve a condom. Summoning the energy, I wait until his eyes are back on me, and I raise my hand and smack my ass.

Luc's cock twitches, and he glares at me. "Fuck, that was naughty." I laugh as he hurries to sheath himself and settles back between my legs.

With his weight pressed on my back and Luc's breath hot in my ear, he growls, "Please tell me I can do that."

"Yes," I hiss, and Luc's body disappears. I brace myself for a spanking, but Luc runs the head of his cock up and down my slick lips. He teases me, and himself, by running it up the crack of my ass, too, his cock nestling between my cheeks while he presses his hips against me and traps it.

"Luc," I beg, tilting my hips up.

"So needy." His voice is strained.

Luc guides himself in, and the press of his perfect cock makes me moan. He eases in and out until everything is wet and frictionless before leaning back over me, pressing a kiss between my shoulder blades. I watch him over my shoulder as his hips move.

Luc's hands are on either side of my body, pressing into the mattress. I curl my hands up and tuck them under my shoulders, tucking my elbows into my chest. Luc's legs stretch out, his weight shifting onto my body more, and his hands slide down, his fingers intertwining with mine. It's a hug from behind, and it slows us, changing the pace.

His hips twist and flex, mine tilt, and soon he's nuzzling the side of my face, breathing hard and still scrambling to be deeper inside of me. The noises I make are quieter, more intimate, but they don't need to be loud. He's right here, absorbing every signal of my pleasure I'm willing to give.

"I'm getting close," he whispers, and I moan. "Can you come like this?"

I can barely shake my head, but I also pull him in tighter. "Don't stop. It feels good."

We're slicked in sweat now, and he slides up my body further, changing the angle. I love the way he feels, pressing against my ass as he grinds into me. Luc backs up just enough to press his face into my back and gives a few harder thrusts before he shatters, pulsing deep inside of me.

Luc rolls off quickly, and I miss his weight and the heat between us. He keeps the momentum and rolls out of bed, back to the bathroom to take care of the condom.

I know I should get up and clean myself, but I'm happy to bask in the best sex I've ever had.

Having a one-night stand with my fake fiancé was the best decision I ever made.

13

Tessa

My internal clock wakes me up, and the first thing I see is the diamond ring on my finger. Last night, after Luc came back to bed, we talked. I told him no one had ever licked my ass like that, and I teased him for not spanking me while he had the chance, and then we wrestled and squirmed on the bed until he landed two gentle swats to my ass.

Then we stayed up way too long talking. I'm always awake early, and my body doesn't care that it's barely slept. I want to stay in bed, but I have to get up and move on: give Luc the ring back to end our fake engagement and say goodbye to my besties.

Luc is still sleeping hard next to me. I would guess as a rideshare driver and a bartender, Luc's schedule has him up late and sleeping through the morning.

I dress quietly, and then, once my things are gathered, I hem and haw over waking Luc up.

Last night—er, this morning, I guess—was fun but also bittersweet. I want us to have more time together, I want him to slap my ass during sex, I want to play with him more doing things I've never done.

I spend a few moments admiring his lean body, relaxed and splayed out and careless, the permanent rosiness of his cheeks, the way his thin lips relax and pout in his sleep. The duvet is pushed to the side, too warm for the summer evening, and I thank Europeans for not bothering with flat sheets. Luc's body is exposed to the air and my eyes.

My phone buzzes in my hand. I'm late to do the walk of shame to brunch, and Jade doesn't hesitate to remind me.

JADE

Woman! I want to see your well-fucked ass before I leave! Don't miss brunch!

EMMA

I have your cardigan and a pair of flip flops.

"Hey, Luc?" I press a hand to his chest, the small smattering of blonde chest hair right above his heart. He stirs but doesn't wake, so I shake his shoulder and speak up. "Luc!"

He blinks and stretches like a cat, his hand sliding down over abs and happy trail, and I think, *hello, I could go for another round*, but then I realize he's fallen asleep again, this time lightly gripping his dick. I bend over and kiss his cheek. "You won't remember this, but I'll message you. Thanks for the great night."

Part of me wants to wake him up, say a real proper goodbye, but the other part tells me it's easier to end a one-night stand if I can't get sucked back into Luc's easy smiles and charm. I straighten and reluctantly pull off the ring, silently thanking Luc's grandmother for letting me borrow it.

The trip to the café will take me only fifteen minutes—god bless the Paris Metro. On the subway, I pull out my phone to send Luc a message. I have five percent of my battery left, so I better make it quick. I type and delete, type and delete, type and delete until it gets to three percent.

How does one end a one-night stand?

I pick the most straightforward option.

TESSA

> I had a great night. Thank you for fond memories of Paris.

I memorize directions to the café—it's only three blocks away—and tuck my phone back in my purse, exiting the metro and briskly walking to brunch. Our table is inside, and the greeting this morning is much more subdued. We give each other kisses on the cheek, à la the French, and I moan in gratitude when I take my heels off and slide into my flip-flops. Emma looks especially tired, and no one has ordered mimosas or wine. There is already a coffee waiting for me, though, and Jade and Emma have coffee, too, while Sara sips her tea.

"You three look . . ." I don't finish the sentence, and Sara chuckles.

"These two,"—she hooks her thumb at Jade and Emma—"drank two bottles of wine back at the room."

My butt hits the seat. "You did?"

"You had some, too," Jade argues to Sara.

"I had one glass."

"And I have a hangover," Emma mumbles.

Jade turns her attention to me and summons up the energy to smirk. "How was your evening?"

Sara puts her chin in her hands and bats her eyelashes at me.

Emma rolls her eyes. "We don't have to tell you everything, Jade."

"Tessa likes a post-orgasm discussion," Jade argues. It's true, though usually, I'm the one listening to Jade dissect her nocturnal—or diurnal, depending—activities with people.

We've always swapped stories or advice since, usually, we're the only two of the group having sex, but in the back of my mind, there's always the drive to normalize healthy, responsible sex for everyone—Sara, Emma, and their grown kids.

I rub Emma's back in sympathy. "Well, I did some things I've never done before," I say.

Jade leans in, eyes wide and ready to listen to everything. "Oh, oh, oh. Did he tie you up? Or, or . . . gah, my brain is too hungover to think of other kinky shit."

"Well, we all know what Jade likes now." Sara smirks.

"It was light butt stuff," I say, shrugging a shoulder. Certainly not as adventurous or kinky as some of the stuff Jade has done over the years that I've known her, but way more daring than I'd done in any previous relationship, never mind a relationship that only lasted a weekend.

But maybe that's the point. Luc and I both knew we would not see each other again; our fake relationship was over, and we could just enjoy the night.

"What are we talking about? Fucking? Fingering? Licking? Smacking?"

"Jade," Emma hisses at her, glancing at the nearby tables.

"The last two," I say.

"Did you like it?" Jade asks, cocking her head. It's completely free of judgment, and I want to talk to Jade about it more. But I know Emma would rather not discuss things like that in public, and I'm only moderately comfortable with it because we're in a quiet corner booth.

"I did." I pick up my menu and change the subject. "Let's talk about it later, though. We should discuss our next weekend together."

They let the conversation change, and between ordering brunch and its arrival, we decide to meet again in Rome in five weeks. Emma's going to live with Jade in Madrid until her business school program starts, so they'll travel together to Rome, where we'll spend a weekend before she moves into student housing.

Jade bemoans the fact that she has to go back to work tomorrow. "I wish I could take time off to show you around Madrid, Emma."

"It's fine," Emma says, shaking her head. "It'll be good for me to explore a city by myself."

"You'll love the museums," I say. "Be sure to check out the Prado. Oh, and they do this ultra-thick hot chocolate that is to die for. I know it's still hot out, but it's worth it, anyway."

By now, we're done eating, and Sara checks her watch. They've got trains to catch, and I need to get to the airport.

We walk back to the hotel, and Jade loops her arm through mine. "Are you going to see Luc again?"

I sigh. "No. It was just one night."

One amazing night.

14

Luc

I WAKE UP, AND THE BED IS COLD, THE HEELS AND DISCARDED dress have disappeared, and my grandmother's ring is on the bedside table. I'm up earlier than normal, and I wonder if she had just left, but then shake my head. It's after noon, and I know she was meeting with the rest of the women for brunch, and then her flight is in the late afternoon.

There's a message from Tessa, so formal and final. But I haven't gotten to say my piece.

I call, but it goes straight to voicemail.

The more time I spend with her, the more sure I am that we have something special, something that's so much more than the engagement we've been pretending.

I jump out of bed, tangle my feet in the duvet on the floor, but manage to right myself before I fall. I throw on clothes. Not my tour uniform, not clothes worth more than I make all week, but pants, a T-shirt, and my favorite pair of shoes.

Where are my keys? I look around my crummy apartment, trying to locate them. I try to ignore the voice in the back of my head telling me that in the light of day, my flat looks worse than last night. Did Tessa look around this morning in the bright daylight and see how rough it is?

It's not that she made me feel bad about my place. She took it in stride, but I think about the hotel they were staying in and that Tessa stayed the night with me.

I hope she thought the sex was worth it. I sure did.

Finally, I find my keys, which were somehow kicked under a chair last night, and head downstairs, stepping onto the street. I know that Tessa's flight isn't until later, but a sense of urgency fills me anyway. She might check out early or catch some last-minute sightseeing with her friends.

I run, which is ridiculous because I have to wait for the metro, and now I'm sweating again, but once I emerge back onto the street by her hotel, I break out into a run again, all the while thinking about how I can convince a smart, driven, career woman to take a chance on me.

When I round the corner and can see the hotel, I slow down. The burst of air conditioning that hits me when the doors open feels refreshing but brings into relief that I'm sweaty again.

I ask the front desk to call her room since I don't have a key card to get into the elevator, but there's no answer. It's early enough that perhaps they haven't checked out yet, so I sit in a chair in the lobby and pull out my phone.

LUC

Thank you for helping with the clothes yesterday. I'll come by this afternoon and leave them at the cleaners near your house.

MÉMÉ

Anything for you. How was your date last night?

LUC

Great.

I smile, thinking about Tessa last night. Her trip to Paris didn't come out as she expected at all, but she stood up for herself and has amazing friends who supported her.

LUC

You'd like her a lot.

MÉMÉ

Do I get to meet her?

I don't have an answer for that, not ready to admit that I may never see Tessa again, so I exit the app and distract myself with a game until I hear familiar voices at the door.

Tessa and her friends stride in, sunglasses on, and everyone but Tessa is dressed casually. She's still in that dress, the black dress that I pushed up last night and revealed that G-string . . .

I snap my thoughts out of the gutter and stand, putting my phone into my pocket. The group hasn't noticed me yet, so I move to intercept them on their way to the elevator.

Jade spots me first and breaks into a huge grin. Her focus draws the attention of the rest of them, and I get to see surprise and pleasure flash across Tessa's face.

It gives me hope.

"Luc, what are you doing here?" She's rosy from the warm day, and there's a flush creeping up her chest. It's from the heat, but I can only think of last night.

Emma herds the other two women toward the elevator to give us some privacy, but Jade stretches onto her toes to call out, "Good job last night!"

Tessa blushes. My grin can't be contained, and I pull Tessa toward me with my hands on her hips. "I want to see you again."

Her smile fades. "What?"

I repeat myself. "I want to see you again. We have great chemistry and connection. You feel it too, no?" A little wrinkle has shown up between her eyebrows, and her mouth has parted in surprise, and I smile even harder at her confusion.

It would be enough to make other men doubt themselves, and I know that there are a lot of hurdles to overcome to see her again, but I'm also an optimist.

"That's . . ." She laughs in disbelief. "I wasn't looking for anything else. I'm not . . . I don't want romance."

"Ah, Tessa," I say, leaning into her and letting my teasing words whisper over her cheek. "Did you think this was a weekend fling? I am your fiancé, after all." I pull back and affect a look of mock hurt.

"Stop it. You know exactly what this was." She shakes her head, but she's still laughing. "We can't be a couple."

"Why not?"

"Well, for starters, I am going to live in Portugal—"

"A two-and-a-half-hour flight."

"—And you work weekends and I work business hours—"

"My schedule is flexible."

"—And I'm like a decade older than you." She pauses and considers that thought. "Wait. I'm forty-two. How old are you?"

I say nothing, letting my smile grow again, and Tessa's eyes widen in horror. "Dear god, you aren't in your twenties, are you?"

I laugh. "No, I'm thirty-one."

Her hands come up to cover her cheeks, which have flushed more with every counterargument I make, and her eyes focus somewhere over her shoulder. "Eleven years younger than me. Oh god."

I pull one hand away so I can see her face and try to draw her attention back to mine. "Age is just a number, yes?"

When she doesn't answer, I tug gently, wrapping my fingers around her wrist. "I like you. You're beautiful and sexy, and I have fun with you."

Her eyes are back on me again, and hope flutters in my chest; possibly more than just asking a woman out—a woman I've already slept with and spent an amazing weekend flirting with—should inspire.

Tessa's eyes dim. "I like you too, Luc. But . . ."

She doesn't know how to finish the sentence, doesn't know how to admit the fear that I see lurking behind her eyes. I think of the Tessa who had dreams of romantic gestures in front of the Eiffel Tower and who was mad at herself for acting petty. She thinks she's missed her chance at love, that her age is holding her back, making her a person she's not ready to be yet.

"You're not ready," I say, understanding. I turn her wrist in my grip, bringing the back of her hand up to my mouth and pressing a kiss to her knuckles. The sadness in her eyes at the gesture cements my belief: Tessa's trying to push romance out of her life when she should do the opposite. She needs to be reminded that there *is* romance in the world, and there's romance for her. Combined with our chemistry, the heat of last night, and the warring feelings in her gaze, I know that this isn't over. "When you are, I'll be there."

15

Tessa

Luc lets go of my hand and steps back. "Ladies," he says, raising his voice to address Jade, Sara, and Emma, who have been lingering nearby. "It was a pleasure meeting you all."

He offers them each kisses on their cheeks, and they say goodbye. I'm afraid that Luc has an aspect to him that I didn't realize was so strong—he's a romantic. Despite my refusal, the spark never left; there was still that hitched-up smile, flirtatious tone, and appreciative eyes.

Case in point: he turns to me and gives me his devastating smile, the corners crinkling. He winks. "I'll see you soon."

Before I can say goodbye, he turns and walks out of the lobby. I watch him for a moment, and then the empty door and the space he occupied before my friends pulling in close, and I shake myself off.

"Okay, let's go pack. We don't have much time left."

"Tessa . . ." Sara begins, but when her thought stalls, she glances at Jade and Emma.

I expect Jade to wrap her arms around my shoulders and lead us toward the elevator, cracking a joke about how *she*

99

was supposed to be the one hooking up this weekend and making a remark about the next guy she's going to set her sights on, but instead, she looks at me with so much concern and asks, "Are you okay?"

"It's fine. I'm fine, I swear." There's too much peppiness in my voice, but I'm not ready to talk about Luc. "It's just the end of a fling. I swear, I didn't catch feelings. I promise."

Despite my tone, the levity doesn't hit, and the air is still heavy with concern. "Sara," I say, threading my arm through hers and tugging her with me as I march forward, "what are you going to do with Zoe tonight?"

She's staying one night in Munich near her daughter before she moves out to Baden-Baden, her home for the next six months. If there's one thing that can distract Sara, it's talking about Zoe.

We pack and talk about their plans and then what Emma and Jade are going to do in Madrid first. Jade describes her three favorite restaurants in her neighborhood, and we debate which one Emma should choose until we're out at the entrance to the hotel.

"Okay," I say. "This is it!" All three of them are headed to the train station, and I'm going to the airport.

The hugs are tight, the emotions close to the surface as I say goodbye. We won't see each other for another month. This is the ending of our weekend in Paris, but the beginning of an entire year living hours away from each other, of new experiences and a foreign home.

"I want pictures of tonight from all of you," I tell them.

"You too," Jade says. "We want to see your new apartment and hear all about Tavira."

There are two cabs waiting, and I get in mine, alone again.

———

THE BOXES I SHIPPED OVER FROM THE STATES WAIT FOR ME IN MY new apartment. It's furnished with two bedrooms. It's also self-check-in, so I wander through the apartment by myself. One bedroom has a small bed and a desk in it, so that's going to be my office.

There's no air conditioning, a fact that, after living in Texas for so long, will take getting used to. I open the windows and the door to the Juliet balcony that overlooks the street, letting fresh air in. The kitchen is compact, tucked into an interior room of the house, and since I like to cook, that's my least favorite part. But the reason I picked this place is the main terrace off of the living space, which has retractable shades and a view of rooftops and the ocean.

I have a lot that I need to do: unpack, grocery shop, set up my new office. But the host left a bottle of wine out—*not* a rosé, a vinho transmontano—and the evening is lovely, so I uncork the full-bodied red wine and sit out on the terrace to watch the sunset.

I'm halfway through my generous pour when my phone buzzes with a message. It buzzes again and again, notices filling up my screen.

SARA

Just got to Zoe's place! Had a great
weekend, ladies.

Then there's a picture sent from Jade, a selfie of her and Emma with a huge skillet of paella between them.

JADE

Emma picked paella for dinner tonight. We
both agreed that we wouldn't make it to a
normal Spanish dinner hour after all that
travel, so we're going to have an early dinner
and then our first night of a month-long
pajama party!

How's your place Tessa?

TESSA

> I'm at my Airbnb. It's nice - clean and spacious and I've got a terrace!

I send a photo of my view, and they send back compliments, but then the chat dies down. They're busy with other things.

I stay up too late putting my apartment together, setting up my office, and adding the few touches of home that I brought with me. The furniture is practical and impersonal, so I make a list of items I want to buy to spruce it up a bit. Jade has an obsession with polaroid pictures and always has a corkboard above her desk with dozens of pictures tacked to it. I stole the idea and hang a board up on my wall. I put up a few pictures: the four of us out touring Paris, some pictures from back in Texas.

I wish I had a photo with Luc, if only to remember the way he made me feel.

16

Luc

IT'S BEEN A FEW DAYS SINCE TESSA LEFT, AND I NEED A distraction. She needs time, and I need to think about something else instead of her. Besides, it's the first afternoon I have had free, and I need to return the outfit I wore to Siempre.

I pick a cleaner near Mémé's apartment and Bernice's shop and then, after prepaying for the cleaning, knock on my grandmother's door.

"Luc!" she says when she opens it. "What a treat." She says that every time I stop by.

I kiss her cheek in greeting and come in. "Have you eaten yet?" There's a new book on the coffee table, and the smell of cigarettes in the air.

She waves me into her kitchen, and together we set out a spread of cold meats and cheeses. Mémé makes tea while I slice a baguette. She tsks when I pull down the Nutella and ignore the jams.

"How was your night?" she asks, dunking the tea bag.

"Loud. Fun. We only had to deal with her ex and his fiancée for a little while. Mostly we danced."

While we eat, I tell her about the club and the rest of the evening up until we left, of course. Mémé, like usual, doesn't eat a lot, but I'm hungry, so my story is dragged out while I eat.

"Are you going to see her again?" Mémé asks over the rim of her teacup.

"I want to."

She tilts her head, studying me. "You like her."

"Yes. But she's living in The Algarve, and when I ask if I can see her again, she gives me excuses."

"What is the line? Maybe she's not that into you?"

I shove a piece of bread in my mouth instead of arguing.

"Couldn't you fly to visit her? It's not far."

"I'd have to take time off work and time away from you. Plus, the costs of flying . . ."

Mémé sighs. "You never make it easy on yourself, do you? Too many jobs—"

"I learned from you."

She points at me, squinting. "—too many women that don't live here, the insistence on getting your own apartment when you could easily live with me."

"You deserve space," I insist. I'd lived with Mémé up until a few months ago. All it took was one time walking in on my grandmother with a man over to realize that I was well past due for having my own place.

"When am I going to see it?"

I groan inwardly. I can't put this off much longer. "I'm still getting settled in."

She waggles a finger at me. "You've put it off long enough. Come on."

She stands and dumps the rest of her tea into the sink.

"What? Now?"

"Yes, now. Enough pushing it off. Let's go." Mémé pokes me with a stern finger like she used to do, finding the sensitive spot under my armpit that normally makes me laugh and run away. But this time, I grab her hand and stay serious.

"It's fine, Mémé. It's just an apartment."

She squints at me. "Is your apartment a shithole?"

I choke on air. "That's not—it's not that bad."

"Don't lie to me." She stares at me for a moment and then spins on her heel. "I need a cigarette." Mémé doesn't smoke in front of me much, and she knows my stance on her smoking, but we've come to a truce about it. She settles into her chair by the front window, which is open.

"Your apartment is a mess, you work three jobs, and you are worried about paying for plane tickets to Portugal. Don't you have savings?"

"I have emergency savings."

"Hmm... I guess it would be bad financial advice to call young love an emergency."

I choke on my wine. "We're not in love," I insist. "I just . . . like her. A lot."

"But not enough to fly to Portugal."

"I want to go," I say. "Visiting her is not entirely about the money."

"Okay." Mémé gestures with her cigarette. "One problem at a time. Go into my bedroom. There's a shoebox on the dresser. Bring that out here."

I obey her orders. The shoebox is light in my hands; there definitely aren't shoes in it.

When I set the box down in front of her, she reaches her hands across the table. I take her hands in mine, and she gives me a small smile. "I know that when you came to live with us, money was tight. I can't imagine how your home life before coming to us affected you. But you need to stop worrying about me. I'm careful with money and living well within my means now."

"Well within your means? But you're always saving food

and containers and shoe boxes," I gesture at the one in front of me.

"I do those things because I want to. My mother lived through the depression, and many of her habits were useful when your grandfather was spending more than we were making. But those habits served me well. When he passed, and I worked at the shop, I saved money in a lot of ways. Not wasting things is one of them."

"I always liked that you never wanted to waste food," I admit. "Your habits have become mine, too."

"But," Mémé chides, "you are taking it too far. If your apartment isn't good enough for me to see, then it's not good enough for you to live in. If your three jobs aren't enough to pay for a trip every once in a while, then we need to evaluate the situation together."

"I can't ask you for help, Mémé."

"I'm not saying you need my help, but maybe you need to help me less. I'll be fine, Luc. I'm healthy and happy, and I know that you will be here to help when I need it. But if I need it, I promise I will ask." She pulls her hands away from mine and pushes the box toward me. "Take this back."

Curiosity sets in as I lift the lid of the box. My eyes widen, and my jaw drops when I catch sight of all the money inside.

"Mémé!"

She shrugs innocently, taking a puff of her cigarette and blowing the smoke out the side of her mouth. "What? Don't think I haven't noticed that you've been leaving money around. I haven't needed it, so I've been saving it for a rainy day."

"This is more than the money I've been leaving behind," I say. My thumb glides over the edges of crisp bills. There must be over a thousand euros in here.

"It is not," she insists. "I had to exchange small bills for bigger ones. You should have seen me at the bank with a stack of damp and wrinkled small bills." She sniffs. "The banker must have thought a new geriatric strip club opened."

That startles a laugh out of me. "This is too much. I can't take this."

"You can and you will. I want you to break your lease immediately. You can move back into your old bedroom."

My eyes prick. For years, I've been focused on the future and how I would take care of my grandmother. That pressure, always in the back of my mind, floods out of me and leaves me feeling . . . not empty, but even more full.

Mémé sees it, snuffs out her cigarette, and stands up, gesturing for me to come to her for a hug. When I stand and fold her tiny frame into my arms, she pats my back and whispers in my ear, "It may be just the two of us, but we take care of each other."

Our hug is long, but it reinforces some of the great things I love about my grandmother. She may be old and not as spry as she once was, but she's tough when it counts.

We pull apart, me wiping my thumbs under my eyes to get rid of the tears and Mémé pulling out a partially used tissue from her sleeve and dabbing her eyes.

"Now, what are you going to do about the girl?"

"Woman," I correct. I let out a breath. "I'm not sure I have many choices."

"Wasn't she here with her friends?"

"Her three best friends, yes."

"What do they think?"

"I haven't asked them."

"We have many motivations for not going for what we want, Luc, but the people who know us best can often see past our own hang-ups. By the sound of it, her friends will either have suggestions or tell you to fuck off. Which do you think it'll be?"

Mémé is right. As protective as Tessa's friends are, they

will tell me if I'm wasting my time. I reach into my pocket, pull out my phone and navigate to Jade's Instagram profile since she's the most active one.

"You know, I've never been to The Algarve. I hear it's lovely." Mémé taps her chin, a twinkle in her eye.

17

———————

Tessa

Sunday, I've got a message in the group chat when I wake up.

EMMA

Good morning. How is everyone today?

That's weird. It was sent two hours ago, and no one has answered. We're way past your typical formalities like this, but I shrug it off.

TESSA

Morning. I'm good.

EMMA

What are your plans for the day?

TESSA

Just getting up and making some coffee.

SARA

How's the local coffee? Maybe you should check out a cafe.

You can people-watch.

Like maybe here?

There's a link to a website, and when I click it, it's a coffee shop just a few blocks from my place.

EMMA

Oh, that place looks good. You should go and see how their coffee is.

TESSA

What's going on?

SARA

We just think you should get out. The weather is nice today, and you've been working hard this week.

TESSA

How do you know the weather is nice?

SARA

I looked at the app. I have all our locations saved.

TESSA

Okay, y'all are being weird but an Americano does sound good so I'm going.

I can't believe I'm putting pants on this early on a Sunday.

If the coffee sucks, I'm blaming you.

JADE

I bet that coffee is really good. And hot. And delicious.

TESSA

Okay. We've officially gone past weird now.

I get out on the street and grudgingly admit that it is a gorgeous day. I'm usually really good about not working on Sundays, but after a week of settling in, I didn't get as much work done as I wanted to. Nothing's urgent, but if I was back at the apartment, I probably would have cracked my laptop open before my coffee had even cooled.

I like the streets here in Tavira. I'm right downtown, minutes from the Gilão River and the Mercado Municipal, where I've been buying my produce. The old buildings are all whitewashed with little embellishments here and there that I've come to love: single buildings tiled in bright blue or painted accents in bright golden yellow and Juliet balconies *everywhere.*

With the weather this nice, I really should get out to one of the beaches today. This region is famous for huge beaches and ginormous cliffs. As I approach the café, my eyes rove over the customers seated outside and . . .

Huh. That guy looks like Luc.

That guy *is* Luc.

He's sitting at a table outside my destination, coffee and pastries in front of him, and an older woman—much older— sitting across from him. He says something to her, making her laugh, and the answering twinkle in his eyes nearly stops my heart.

He glances up and spots me, and his smile somehow contorts to smoldering while still keeping that spark of excitement that makes me feel lit up from my head to my toes. How can this man make me feel so sexy with just a look?

What the hell is he doing here?

As I approach, Luc folds his arms on the table and bites his lip, clearly pleased with himself. With his attention diverted, the woman with him—his grandmother?—carefully turns in her chair to see what he's looking at.

"Luc," I say, trying to keep a sternness in my tone that he absolutely ignores. He rises and kisses my cheeks, muttering a low and affectionate "Tessa," that makes me want to curl up into him.

But I won't. Because that would encourage him.

Before I can reprimand him, Luc offers the woman a hand so she can stand and introduces us. "Tessa, this is my grandmother, Anouk. Mémé, this is Tessa."

The woman leans forward, and we kiss cheeks. "Tessa, it is lovely to meet you," she says in slow, practiced English. Anouk is petite and gray-haired, stylish, and smells faintly of cigarette and perfume.

"My pleasure," I answer in French. "I was not expecting to see you." I direct a glare at Luc, but it's not very stern. It's hard to be when he just grins back at me. "What are you doing here?"

"Please," Anouk gestures to the third chair at the table. "Join us." We sit and get settled in, Luc waving for a server, who takes my order in English before walking off, and we can get back to my question. "I have never been to this part of Portugal before, so we thought we would visit. It's been so long since Luc and I took a trip together, and he's humoring his grandmother."

"A tourist trip? What will you be doing? Surely not waiting around all day, hoping to run into me." Then the lightbulb switches on. "Oh, my friends are in on it, aren't they? You had help."

My coffee comes, and I thank the server, the Portuguese clunky on my tongue. I only know a few words, and I try to use them as much as I can.

"Don't be mad at them. They wouldn't tell me your address and said that if you didn't want to see me, I had to go away, or they'd—" He glances at his grandmother. "Well, let's just say Jade can be graphic and creative with her threats, and Emma was less creative but surprisingly more terrifying."

I shake my head. "They told you where to go for coffee

this morning and then worked together to get me here. I *knew* something was up."

"You don't have to stay," he says, all traces of amusement gone. "I will leave you alone if that's what you want. But . . ." He smiles again. "We're going to walk the beach, visit the fortress, have lunch at the marina, and if there's time, visit the museum. And let me be clear." He leans in, more serious now, and places a chaste hand on my arm. "This is just a friend inviting another friend to have some fun." He thinks for a moment. "With his grandma."

I had just been thinking that if left to my own devices, I would be working, and that defeats the purpose of being here. I *want* to get out and explore the region, and while I can do it on my own . . .

"Okay, I'm in. They were on my agenda anyway," I say, a white lie, though Luc seems like he's trying to keep expectations low. "Where are you staying?"

We talk about their hotel around the corner, and they tell me that they're staying two nights and flying back to Paris on Tuesday. When I've finished my breakfast, Anouk insists on paying for us, and then we walk to the fortress.

On the way, I check my phone.

SARA

I hope you aren't mad at us. It was only a little meddling.

EMMA

He promised he'd behave. And we swear he was going to go anyway, with our help or not, so we were really just narrowing down his search radius so he could find you.

TESSA

I'm not mad. We're sightseeing together. His grandmother is a treat and Luc's offering friendship and not being pushy.

EMMA

Watching Luc as a tourist is an odd flip from our meeting. He's inquisitive, and I find that I miss all the little things he knew about Paris. I want to hear him tell me all the little things about here, too.

He's also adorable with his grandmother. He helps her with stairs and finds her a seat if she gets tired. In fact, that's what she talks about the first time we're alone together, sitting on a bench in a small neighborhood park while Luc runs off to buy a bottle of water for her. While the heat is nothing like Texas, it is an unusually hot day in the low eighties.

"Luc's always been such a hardworking man," she tells me. "Always very good at taking care of me. It's a relief to have him living with me again."

I snap my head up. "Luc moved in with you?"

"Did you see his apartment? Horrifying. He's always wanted to take care of me and got it in his head that I needed space. Moving into that apartment was a mistake in the first place—why pay the extra rent when we were perfectly happy living together? Besides," she leans in to confide with me. "I couldn't reach the top cabinets in my kitchen without him. It nearly halved my storage space to not have him around to reach things for me."

I laugh at that. "Do you cook a lot?"

"Of course. My family is from the maritime region, and while there are plenty of fantastic restaurants in Paris, none of them make our traditional dishes quite like home. Or like home used to," she amends. "Last time I went back to Île de

Ré, it was changed. So touristy, so rich. Not like my childhood."

Luc returns, and after hydrating, we walk the beach—Anouk insists we walk, even though Luc suggests we take a car—to our lunch spot overlooking the marina, where we have a fantastic meal, and Anouk tells me stories from Luc's childhood that have me laughing so hard, I cry while Luc flushes in embarrassment and avoids eye contact with the both of us while muttering French obscenities.

The food is good, the chilled table wine is even better, and I feel a bloom of friendship for Anouk. Afterward, she excuses herself to go back to their hotel and rest, which leaves Luc and me walking together aimlessly.

"Anouk tells me you moved in with her."

"I did," Luc confirms. "I've made some other financial decisions lately that I hope will make things easier."

"Oh?" I say, eyebrow raised. "Like what?"

Luc points at a fishing boat passing by, and we watch it before he gets back to the question. "Mémé has more savings than I thought. I was worried about supporting her throughout her retirement, but it turns out she's frugal not out of necessity but for the sheer desire to be frugal."

Maybe it's because I'm armed with this knowledge, but Luc does seem lighter. He's always given me a sense of a care-free attitude, but his grandmother had been a source of tension. I can see the relief all over his body as he talks about his grandmother now, and wonder how I could have missed the sore spot before.

"That's great," I say.

"While I was slipping her cash every chance I got, she was hoarding it in a safe place for me. When we talked last week, she decided it was time to give me that stash, and I could put it to good use. Treat myself. Like taking her on a trip to the coast to visit a beautiful woman."

His lips tip up with mischievousness, and I laugh, pushing him gently away from me as we walk side by side.

"I thought we were just friends."

"We are. It doesn't change the fact that you're beautiful."

Fortunately, we arrive at our destination, the museum, and I can ignore Luc's words and the flush in my cheeks from his compliments and instead learn about the region's fishing history. It's not sexy, but it's interesting, and that's what I need right now.

I lose track of Luc in the museum, and when I exit, I check my phone for a message from him.

LUC

I'm here. Take your time.

Attached is a map pin that shows his location a few blocks away at a park. I find Luc stretched out in the shaded grass, eyes closed. I stand and watch him for a few moments, the sunlight dappling his skin and the lines of his face relaxed. It reminds me of last weekend when I left him sleeping in bed and the brief chance to admire him in his sleep.

"I was thinking," he says, and I nearly jump out of my skin. Luc cracks one eye open and grins while I press a palm to my chest to slow my racing heart. "I want to take Mémé out somewhere nice for dinner. Maybe I can walk you home, and we can meet up again?"

I like that he's not inviting me to dinner just the two of us. Right? Yes, I like it. I like Anouk, I'm definitely not disappointed.

"That sounds great. Did you have a place in mind?"

He tells me the name, and I look it up. It's a fine-dining restaurant in my neighborhood. The walk to my apartment is brief, and I'm pleased that the area is looking familiar. Luc leaves me with a kiss on the cheek and a promise to pick me up at seven.

When he does, I get another kiss on the cheek and an

appreciative scan of my body. I'm wearing a lavender dress with sheer capped sleeves and my favorite diamond earrings. Luc is in slim-fit pants—charcoal this time—and a white button-up with the sleeves rolled to his forearms. Anouk is at his side in a retro Chanel dress and an accenting pair of flats, and she kisses me, too.

"You look great," I say, stepping back to look at his pants again. They fit him so well they must have been tailored.

"Thank you," he says. "Mémé helped me pick it out."

"Good job," I tell her. "You look lovely, too."

She smooths her hands down her dress and then takes one of Luc's arms. "My friend Bernice is a tailor and owns a consignment shop in our neighborhood. Very convenient when you want to be fashionable on a dime."

Dinner is lovely and friendly. Anouk asks me about my life back in the States, and when I hear a familiar southern twang from a nearby table, Luc strikes up a conversation, and we meet a young couple from Dallas. I drink too much wine, a terras de cister that's been perfectly chilled, and the bubbles go right to my head.

At the end of the evening, Luc puts his grandmother in a car and walks me back to my apartment. I lean on him, liking the way he smells and the heat of his body, even in the summer air.

"Tessa," he murmurs into my hair, and I hum. "We're here."

I raise my head and see that we are, in fact, in front of my building.

"Boo," I say, and my body bounces when Luc laughs. I pivot, resting my chin on his chest and looking up at him. "I have to work tomorrow." I told him I have a meeting every Monday with my staff.

"I know," he kisses my forehead. "I'm going to take Mémé to see the Benagil Caves down the coast. Can I see you for dinner? Do you have time for that?"

"You could come up now," I say, clutching at the side of his shirt.

Luc just smiles at me and kisses my hair again, gently pulling back. He puts a finger under my chin and tilts my head up. I'm expecting a kiss, but instead, I can barely feel his breath against my lips. "I'm not a fling, Tessa." His tone is light and teasing, and he kisses the corner of my mouth. "Ask me a different question."

The words get stuck in my throat, and after a few moments, Luc laughs and eases away from me.

"You've been drinking, too. Sleep it off, and I'll see you tomorrow, ma chouchoute."

I laugh at the term of endearment in French that literally translates to *my little cabbage,* but I don't move. He tilts his chin up. "Go. I'll see you tomorrow."

With one last glance, I turn and enter the building. By the time I get up to my balcony and look down on the street, Luc is gone.

18

Tessa

MY CALL WITH ONE OF MY WRITERS IS RUNNING LONG, AND while her article about her trip to South Africa is interesting, it's not enough to keep my attention from wandering to Luc, who's been messaging me all day while he and Anouk explore the coast. I'm getting pictures of beaches and beautiful cliffs and then Anouk on the bow of a small boat, a life jacket on, and a marina behind her.

"Okay, just two more things, Nikki, and then we're good. Could you explain more about the borders of Kruger Park? Maybe on the second page in the paragraph that starts with 'Unhindered by coastline or the invisible boundaries of country lines . . .'."

"Yup, I can do that," she responds in her posh English accent. She lives in London, and we've already talked about the possibility of getting together when I get the chance to get across the channel.

Whenever that might be. Because if I'm ever going to see Luc again and I have weekend getaways once a month with the ladies, my schedule will be packed.

My phone buzzes with another incoming call, an unknown number, and I click the screen off, sending it to voicemail.

"Good. Our art director asked if you have a photo of the lilac-breasted roller. He thinks that features more prominently than the secretary bird. No big deal if you don't."

She tells me she'll see what she has, and we talk a bit more about her upcoming trips, and then we hang up.

I've got a voicemail, so I click over to listen.

"Tessa, this is Yumi. Can you call me when you get a chance? We need to talk."

My stomach drops. What could my ex's new fiancé possibly want to talk to me about? I had hoped that this would be the end. If I'm lucky, I'll never see James or anyone from that party ever again.

I was counting on just fading away. Who would care whether Luc or I got married or if we broke up?

I try to get back to work, but every time my phone lights up with a notification, I jump, and I realize I just need to bite the bullet and get it over with.

Yumi picks up on the first ring.

"Hello, Tessa."

If there's any anger toward me, I can't hear it in her voice. "Yumi, how are you?" I ask, years of politeness ingrained in me.

Yumi cuts right to the point. "I'm calling to apologize and assure you that I had no idea that James was still dating you."

My eyebrows launch into my hairline. I wasn't expecting that.

"Thank you?"

"You're welcome. You should also know that we broke up. I owe you for that, too. James's invitation to you for the party was pure hubris on his part, and I'm glad it came to bite him in the ass. I'm glad my eyes were opened to his character before I married him."

"That's good." Yumi's matter-of-factness about the whole thing is startling. Almost as startling as her next change of topic.

"How's Luc?"

"Oh. He's good." I feel like she's fishing for something, and I'm not sure what.

"Are you seeing each other?"

"Well, he's actually here now, in The Algarve. But it's complicated."

"Hmm. Complicated or not," Yumi says. "Can you do me a favor?"

"Maybe?"

She chuckles. "This is really petty, but James didn't believe your engagement to Luc was real and obsessed about it." She laughs without any humor. "Red flag, right? I should have known. Anyway, that's not my business whether you're engaged or not, but seeing as how Luc's visiting you, could you maybe post a picture of the two of you on Instagram? James follows both of you with a sock account, and it'll give me a real pleasure to know that he's out there somewhere blowing a gasket over our engagement dissolving and yours thriving."

"You are evil."

Yumi cackles. "He deserves it. It's a small ask, right? One last chance to make him jealous."

"I'll see what I can do," I say.

"And Tessa? If James had looked at me with half as much affection as Luc looks at you, we'd be having a very different conversation. Think about that."

I tell her I will, and then we say goodbye. I sit in my office for a moment, reflecting on the conversation. Bonding with Yumi over James's shitty behavior isn't something I thought I would be doing today.

A notification from WhatsApp pops up on my phone.

LUC

> We are back in Tavira. Mémé slept most of
> the ride back and is exhausted. She's going
> to have a quiet dinner tonight, but I still want
> to see you.

We message back and forth, me telling Luc I don't want to take time away from his grandmother and him insisting that he lives with her and can spend a dinner apart. We finally settle on Luc picking up groceries and bringing them to my place for me to cook dinner.

I'm tidying up my apartment–stuffing the "possibly re-wear" pile of clothes into the hamper and wiping down the bathroom counter–when I get a text from Sara.

SARA

> I HAVE A FUNGUS EMERGENCY.

> Actually, it's an entire apartment emergency!!!
> HELP!

From earlier texts, I know that Emma's out exploring Madrid and Jade's working late, so I'm the only one available.

TESSA

> I'm here! What's your emergency?

The response back is a slew of pictures, including . . . yup, that's mushrooms growing out of the base of a shower stall.

I'm looking at the rest of them—a dingy bathroom, a too-cramped bedroom, a barren kitchen—when I get an incoming video chat request from Sara.

"Hey," I say, and immediately frown at her. She's outside somewhere, her headphones in her ears and what is probably a mug of tea in front of her. Her eyes are red-rimmed, and her jaw is clenched, anger and frustration battling it out for center stage. Alarm rises in my voice. "Where are you?"

"I'm at a café," she says, sniffing. "My apartment is horrible. Horrible, Tessa! There's a huge water stain on the ceiling, and the bedrooms are much smaller than I thought. And the mushrooms! Tessa! I can't live with mushrooms in my bathroom. I like to eat them, not live with them!"

"What happened to the apartment you were going to rent?"

Now that she's focused on talking to me, her emotions have tipped over to anger. "That *was* the apartment. Or, at least, I'm pretty sure it is. It's definitely the same outside picture on the listing, and I spent a good fifteen minutes trying to compare the interior photos to reality and then another ten minutes arguing with the landlord, who *conveniently* doesn't speak English. It's much harder to argue in German when you don't know German."

There's a knock on my door, and I let Luc in. He raises his eyebrow when he sees that I'm on the phone. "Hey Sara, Luc's here." To Luc, I say, "Sara's having a crisis."

His expression morphs into concern, and he sets the groceries down on the counter.

Sara sniffles. "Am I interrupting your date?"

I glance at Luc. She kind of is, but I'm worried. Luc, the sweetheart, reads my expression perfectly.

"Put her on speakerphone," he says.

I disconnect my headphones, and Sara brings him up to speed. I open my laptop and pull the photos Sara messaged us up so that we can see them better.

Luc sucks in air through his teeth. "That does not look good."

"Right?" Sara keeps ranting. "The Wi-Fi is supposed to be good, but I tried to video chat with Zoe, and it was laggy. That's why I'm at this café. That and I had to get out of there. It smells. I'm pretty sure there's meat juice coagulated into the grooves of the refrigerator. I can't sleep there, much less do yoga or eat. How am I supposed to film my video for Wednesday? Oh, you think this is funny?"

"What? No! I'm not laughing." I glance back at my phone, and Sara's looking off-screen at someone else, and now the anger is swapped for humiliation, and her eyes are welling up.

"Oh, sweetie . . ."

Someone says something in the background that's too far away and accented for me to understand through her earbuds, but they're coming closer.

"Well, that's good to know," Sara says in response. "But I don't have a lawyer. Or a grasp of legalese in German. Or a place to live." Her shoulders slump at each point she makes.

I strain to hear more, but it sounds like an adult talking in a Charlie Brown cartoon. I glance at Luc. "Can you understand what they are saying?"

He shakes his head, so I watch Sara's face to try to figure out what's happening.

"Sara, who is that?" I ask.

Her eyes flick to us and then back to the guy. "He's another patron of the café, and he might have a place for me to stay. Tessa, can I call you back?"

"I want a call or text within the next ten minutes," I say sternly, and she blows me a kiss before hanging up.

"I'm so sorry about that," I apologize.

"Please. I like your friends a lot, and Sara needs you. Don't stress about it." He kisses my temple. "Can I pour us some wine?"

"Oh god, yes."

I pull out glasses while Luc uncorks the bottle.

"I feel for Sara," he says. "It's tough when you feel like you have few options for where to live, and none of them are good."

Luc tells me about apartment hunting in Paris and moving out of his grandmother's place while I start to prep dinner. Two minutes later, I get a message from Sara.

SARA

I'm fine. I'm headed back to the (shitty)
apartment. I'm going to look at listings.
Tessa, have a great date with Luc and we
can talk in the morning.

I put my phone down and try to let go of my worry over Sara and focus on Luc. Fortunately, that's easy because Luc turns on the charm, probably to help me distract myself. An hour later, Luc and I are dining out on my patio. I've made a risotto with peas and pancetta, which I serve with roasted vegetables. We have fresh glasses of chilled white wine, which we sip while we eat. Having him in my kitchen was fun. I feel at home when I cook, and I was in a great mood from seeing Luc again. Music was on, I swayed while I cooked, and Luc's gaze gradually shifted from amused to appreciative to hunger.

Even after a delicious meal, the hunger is still there. It feels like a first date, but really, it would be—what? Our ninth if we go by meals, our sixth if we count the days on the calendar?

Never mind that we've already had toe-curling, hot sex.

Our feet are up on the balcony railing, and we've opened a second bottle of wine. The music's still playing in the kitchen through the open doors, and Luc softly hums with it. We're sitting close, his warm toes touching mine and contrasting with the cool metal, and my smile feels dopier, more love-sick when I look at him.

Love-sick?

Ugh. The word is a better fit for a teenager than a grown-ass woman.

"I had an interesting phone call today," I say, swirling my wine as the sky fades from blue to pink. I tell him about my call with Yumi. "What do you think?"

"Sounds petty and manipulative, and I love it. Would I rather punch him in the nose? Sure. But this won't get me arrested." Luc stands, retrieving his phone from the kitchen island. "This is selfish, too," he tells me. "I want photos of us."

He takes several pictures of just me until I cross my eyes and stick my tongue out at him. Then it's sunset and selfies, each one pressing us closer together. I love the way I fit under his arm, and I momentarily forget about the camera and close my eyes, running my nose up the collar of his shirt to his neck.

"Tessa," he says, and it comes out rough and gravelly.

I tilt my head up to look at him as he tilts down, and our lips come crashing together. Luc's arm tightens around my waist, his mouth working mine open and sweeping in with a groan. God, he tastes good, like the crisp wine we're drinking and the warm summer air.

Luc takes the glass out of my hand and, without removing his mouth from mine, places it on the table. Both hands come up into my hair as he walks me back into the apartment. A few steps in, my heels hit the couch, and Luc catches me, breaking our kiss to lay me down and cage me in: hands in my hair, legs between mine, and cock so deliciously hard beneath the denim of his jeans.

Now that we're horizontal, with the press of Luc right where I need him, the pace slows down. Luc's leading, and while the weight of him makes me want more, faster, harder, now, I can practically hear him remembering that there's a reason he didn't want to kiss me.

I half-expect him to stop, but he doesn't. It's slow and languid, and while he traces parts of me with his fingers like he's cataloging my contours, his hands don't wander south.

Not even to my ass, and I want to ask if he's feeling okay. But not enough to stop the kissing.

My hands can barely move, so focused on keeping him here and not letting him pull away. I moan when Luc shifts, and the pressure of his cock against me rubs just right, but I also love the flex of muscle and the heat of his skin under my grip.

I don't know how long we kiss. I haven't made out this much—or dry-humped like this—in at least twenty years. It shocks me that I've forgotten that such a simple, relatively chaste thing could feel so good.

But eventually, Luc pulls back. "I should go." The words are muttered against my ear, the breathing ragged and the tone reluctant.

"Stay," I plead. I don't want this to end, and I know that a build-up like this can only lead to something even more amazing than the night we've already spent together.

Luc kisses me again, and I think for a moment that I'll win, but then he pulls away. "I have to go," he says. "Our flight is early in the morning, and I need to take care of my grandmother."

I'm tempted to offer him my guest room, the couch, to ask for just five more minutes like a child, but I don't. Luc leans down quickly, surprising me, putting us nose to nose. His eyes are wide open, feral, and his lips kiss-swollen. "Don't ask me to stay, Tessa. Don't beg. Just ask me another question."

I could easily ask him for something else. Ask him to date me, ask him to be my boyfriend, whatever would change his mind and make him stay.

But even I can realize that I'm so full of sexual frustration right now that I might make a promise I can't keep.

Instead, like a coward, I say, "Five more minutes?"

There's a flash of hurt in Luc's eyes and a pang of guilt in my chest. He hides it quickly, though, and presses down, giving me a quick, chaste kiss.

"I'll text you in the morning when I'm on my way to the airport. I'll come see you next weekend, ma chouchoute. And every Sunday until you tell me to give up."

Luc casts one last look of longing back at me before the

door snicks shut. I want to melt into a puddle, both from frustration at myself and from the ache between my legs that makes me want to strip and pull out my trusty vibrator. It's not like I haven't been using it and pretending I don't think about Luc when I do.

Screw it. The vibrator is too far.

I unbutton my jeans and shove them down, thrusting my hand into my panties. Two seconds later, I'm coming, my thighs quivering and clenching around my hand, just as the door swings open.

"Tessa, lock me out—" Luc's jaw drops. "Oh fuck." His hands cover his face, then rifle through his hair. "Fuck, fuck, Tessa!"

I can only laugh as he spins around and shuts the door behind himself again.

"Tessa!" he shouts through the door. "Lock me out."

"Okay, okay," I say, getting up. With the hand that hasn't been down my pants, I lock the door.

"Thank you." The words are muffled through the door.

"Goodnight, Luc."

There's quiet for a moment, and then a muttered expletive and the shuffling of feet as Luc finally leaves.

I wash my hands and change into pajamas, and finally, pick up my phone. The first new message, about an hour ago, was from Sara. There's a selfie of her looking rather disgruntled with a guy with a blond man bun and sharp cheekbones wearing sweats. There's also a photo ID of the same guy, plus a phone number and address.

JADE

Um, Sara, who are you stalking?

SARA

This guy, Chris, has a room for me to rent.

JADE

Wait, what happened to your apartment?

Sara filled Jade, and eventually Emma, in on the fungus-and-mold situation. They've been weighing the pros and cons of the apartment, stranger danger versus the kindness of humanity.

TESSA

What do we know about this guy?

SARA

I searched online but his name is common so the results are mostly about an MP in Britain's Parliament and a goth-punk rockstar.

Wait, how was your date with Luc? Is he still there?

TESSA

It was great. He's back at his hotel.

JADE

Did your date end with a bang?

TESSA

Jade, focus. Sara's housing crisis.

JADE

Yes, right, sorry.

SARA

I can't believe I'm doing this, but I'm taking Chris up on it.

EMMA

Are you sure? I know odds are tiny that he would hurt you, but still. Is it worth the risk? You could just come here.

Jade's brushing her teeth right now, but she says there's room, and she'd love to have you.

But she's also asking if Chris is as cute in person as in the pictures.

WHICH IS NOT A FACTOR.

TESSA

It's going to be fine. Just keep us up to date.

EMMA

If anything feels off, dial 112 first.

SARA

Did you just look up the 911 equivalent for Germany?

EMMA

Well, I wasn't sure if it was the same in every European country.

How are you getting to his place?

SARA

He's picking me up. Stay tuned.

Oh, and the cherry on the fucking cake of this shit-hole apartment? They're blaring death metal. It's ten o'clock at night!

JADE

Sara's dropping f-bombs???

Do you need to do some breath-focusing exercises?

SARA

Even I'm not THAT good.

The bass is dropping ceiling dust in the kitchen.

TESSA

Face it, you would be terrified to eat anything you made in there.

SARA

True.

I'm nervous, distract me. Tessa, on a scale of one to ten, how was your date with Luc tonight?

TESSA

An eight.

SARA

What would have made it a ten?

JADE

Sex.

Hahaha, Emma just muttered "it's always sex with you".

SARA

Okay, Chris is here.

I just got in the backseat like a weirdo. As if he's an Uber driver. I think he's laughing at me.

EMMA

Share your location with us!

I move into my office and turn my laptop back on so I can track her progress. I'm also trying not to obsess in thinking about Luc. What would have made the date a ten? My first thought when Sara asked was not sex or Luc staying the night but a commitment. Like maybe, if I'd gotten the courage to ask Luc to be with me, it would have been perfect.

SARA

He's staying on the right route so far.

We're leaving the city limits.

I wish it was daylight so I could see where we were going. I should have called earlier.

I'm super unsure if I'm creeped out because of some gut instinct or if it's just because the German countryside is creepy at night.

Um

We made it.

EMMA

Um? What does that mean?

Sara doesn't answer for a while, and I distract myself by getting ready for bed instead of worrying about my best friend a thousand miles away.

EMMA

SARA!

SARA

Sorry, sorry. Everything's fine. The house is a freaking mansion. It's really nice. Chris showed me right to a guest bedroom and I have an ensuite and everything.

There are goddamn tassels on the duvet and decorative pillows.

Chris does not look like a duvet and decorative kind of guy.

TESSA

Is he married?

SARA

I don't know. I didn't even think about that.

Yikes. Is there going to be a wife downstairs tomorrow at breakfast? Awkward.

Okay, I'm literally exhausted, so I'm going to bed.

EMMA

Lock your bedroom door! Just in case.

SARA

It's got a deadbolt, actually. Maybe this place is a rental? IDK, I'll explore tomorrow. Good night!

There's a flurry of goodnight messages, and I close my laptop, satisfied that Sara is safe for now.

With her settled, I get into bed, and my thoughts turn back to Luc. Sara's trusting a stranger with her life. Why can't I trust Luc with my heart?

19

Luc

I GET THE LOW BATTERY WARNING ON MY PHONE AROUND THREE o'clock on Saturday, five days after seeing Tessa. "Shit," I mutter under my breath and glance at my passenger in the rearview mirror and hope that they didn't hear me. It's a short ride, so once I drop them off, I stay at the curb and fiddle with my phone. I remove the plug from my phone and reinsert it. No charge. I trace the wire back to the center console and the built-in USB plug and press it in further. Nothing.

"Crap," I say, slumping my head against the steering wheel. Either there's something wrong with the plug or my cord, and I hope it's the latter. I don't have much time—I have my shift at the bar tonight and then my flight to see Tessa in the morning—so I need to get my phone charging. I might even have time for one more ride if I hustle.

I'm close to Mémé's—I mean, my place—so I flick my turn signal on, navigate back into traffic, and in twenty minutes, I'm pulling into a spot not far from our place.

I take the stairs two at a time and fling the door open. "Mémé," I call out. "I just need a new phone cord."

"Luc?"

Mémé's voice makes my blood freeze; it's weak and flecked with pain.

"Mémé?" I rush around the corner. She's not in the sitting room. There's a shuffling noise, and when I turn my head toward the kitchen, I see her arm outstretched on the kitchen floor. "Mémé!"

She's sprawled out on the wood floor, in a position that can't be comfortable, and I crash down to my knees at her side, fear choking my insides like a vise. "Mémé, what happened? Are you okay?"

"I fell. Just lost my balance and fell."

I pat my pockets for my phone before realizing that it's out in the car and possibly dead. "Where's your phone? I'm going to call for an ambulance."

Mémé directs me to it, and in a few moments, I'm on the phone with an operator, following instructions and asking Mémé questions while help is on the way. Her answers have my worry escalating; it hurts to move, and she doesn't know if she hit her head.

I ride with her in the ambulance, and then it's a slog of waiting: waiting for a doctor to talk to her, waiting for scan results, waiting for more information. I remember to call the bar and let them know I won't be coming in, but as the day slips into darkness, I realize I'm not going to make my flight. I don't have Tessa's number, and my phone is in my car, dead. I try to log into my Instagram account, but thanks to two-factor authentication, I can't get in.

I just can't worry about it right now.

I snooze by Mémé's bedside, being startled awake in the morning when a new doctor comes in to check on her. "Good morning, everyone. How are we feeling today?"

"Okay," Mémé says, and my heart sinks at the tiredness in

her voice.

"You don't have a concussion; you passed the night with gold stars. How's that cast feeling?" The staff did a full evaluation on my grandmother and discovered that aside from the back pain—thankfully muscle injury and not bone—and the concern over a head injury, Mémé had also landed on and broken her arm. It wasn't bad enough that anyone, Mémé included, had noticed until a nurse had asked her to press down in a series of tests, and Mémé had winced.

"Just fine."

The doctor inspects her cast, checks her vitals, and pronounces that the back injury is going to require some physical therapy, and they're going to move her to another ward. She'll stay a few more days under supervision until she can stand up on her own.

We wait again until Mémé has a room, the staff has moved her in, she's met her new medical team, we've signed paperwork, and all the other monotony of the medical system.

Once we're alone again, Mémé turns to me. "Darling, I'm so sorry you had to miss your flight."

"It's fine, Mémé."

"Have you talked to Tessa?"

"No, not yet. I'll call her when I get home."

"You should go now," Mémé urges. "The excitement is over, and the boring stuff begins. I'm sure you don't want to watch me exercise or whatever horrid thing they'll have me doing. Then you can get a good night's sleep and be back tomorrow."

"Are you sure?"

"Absolutely. I've got my phone, so I'll call you if I need anything." She pauses. "Actually, call me before you come back here. I might have you bring a few things for me."

I shake my head, upset I didn't think about what things she would want to have with her for a multiple-day stay. "Of course."

"Good," she says, and then gestures me over to kiss her cheek and gives me a gentle shove—with her good arm—toward the door.

The sun blasts me in the face as I step out of the hospital. I have no idea what time it is, but I can guess that it's near sunset, and I wonder what Tessa did this morning when I didn't meet her at the café. I take the metro toward home, guilt hanging over me that I was going to spend every Sunday in Portugal with Tessa. What was I thinking? What if Mémé had fallen twenty-four hours later, and I'd been away? This time, I was going to stay for two days, flying in Sunday morning and out Monday night. Mémé would have been on the floor for who knows how long.

Hell. I was going to go right from driving to the bar. Mémé easily would have been on the floor all night if not for my stupid, wonderful phone cord.

I'm blinded by the sun again as I step out of the metro station and point my feet toward home. The streets are busy with the market nearby, and the temperature dipped down just enough to promise the end of summer and the bustle of Sunday night diners.

The apartment is empty and dark when I get in. I plug my phone in and tackle the dirty dishes and the food left out on the counter.

When my phone is charged enough to turn on, it dings with missed calls, voicemails, and text messages. A quick glance shows most of them are from Tessa.

I slump into the armchair in the living room. Forty-eight hours ago, the thing I wanted more than anything was for Tessa and me to be together. Mémé's fall has turned that into wishful thinking. I can't leave my grandmother now. I can't fly to visit Tessa every weekend. I know Tessa needs time to trust me, to heal from the hurt James caused her, but I don't have the time.

My heart aches knowing I have to let Tessa go.

20

Tessa

Throughout the week, Sara has been updating us on her bizarre living situation.

He smokes! At least he always does it outside.

I'm guessing he is not married. The inside of his refrigerator is like a textbook sad bachelor's diet.

I have literally accomplished all my goals for the day and Chris isn't even awake yet.

Basically, they are complete opposites, and Sara has free run of the house. Chris has an entire wing where he spends most of the day and comes out with ink-stained fingers. There's artwork all over the place, and he's got a broody, contemplative mood most of the time, which fits since Sara has discovered he's an artist.

It's a great distraction since Luc is very late to meet me at the café and is not answering his phone. I don't know if he missed his flight or if it's something worse like he was in a car accident last night while driving or . . .

Or he realized he couldn't do the long-distance thing.

Or that I'm too old for him.

But he would call, right? Luc, kind, thoughtful Luc, wouldn't just not show up.

I give up waiting and send Luc another text, asking him to call me. When I get back to my apartment, I pull up the group chat.

TESSA

I'm worried about Luc.

He's not here yet. What if he's given up?

Dots appear and disappear as my friends type, but no messages come in. My heart clenches, and I chew on my lower lip. Do they think he's given up, too?

The phone buzzes in my hand, but it's not a message, it's a group video call. I answer, and the screen fills with Emma, Sara, and Jade's faces.

"Luc has not given up on you," Jade says firmly.

I'm surprised by how sure she sounds. "How do you know?"

"He's crazy about you. We can all tell."

Sara and Emma agree.

"It just doesn't make sense."

There's silence after my confession, and then Emma speaks softly. "James really did a number on you, didn't he?"

I close my eyes. These ideas about myself have been rattling around in my head for quite some time, but it takes courage to unravel them and pull them out, even to my best friends, people who I know, undoubtedly, have my best interest at heart.

"What if this is it for me? What if I'm just never supposed to get married?"

"Tessa." Jade's voice is filled with sympathy.

"When I turned forty, I gave up. I thought if it hadn't happened by then, then it probably wouldn't happen. If I was destined to be single my whole life, then I might as well accept it."

Someone hums, and they wait for me to keep going.

"And I did. You know what they say; love finds you when you stop looking. Sure enough, there was James. Divorced and a friend of the family and successful and good-looking. I thought, finally, finally! He looked so good on paper, right? We had so much in common, and he seemed perfect."

Looking back, I wonder if I moved our relationship along too quickly because I thought the whole thing was a miracle. Maybe I went in with my expectations far too high.

"Are you worried it's not going to last again?"

"I'm worried that I'll get my hopes up, and it feels worse every time. And Luc, he's young and optimistic. What future does he even see in me? I just want to protect him from all the heartbreak I had."

"You can't, though," Jade says. "He's a grown man. He's in his thirties!"

"Barely."

"Do you remember us at that age? We'd already had heartbreak and loss and our biggest fears realized."

Jade's right, of course. Between the four of us, we'd gone through our own fair share of trauma, from Jade's cancer to Sara losing her husband to parents and friends dying.

"No one's hung up on Luc's age except you," Emma says. "Let Luc pave his own way. If it leads to heartbreak, that's just part of life, and you can't protect him from that. What if it doesn't? You deserve love. I promise you are too young to give it up."

Sara chimes in. "Besides, looking good on paper doesn't mean squat. On paper, James seemed perfect. On paper, my apartment looked perfect."

"Perfect on paper lies," Jade adds.

"I took a leap of faith by getting into a stranger's car," Sara continues. "I know it's not a perfect analogy because it was high risk, and I was just trying to find a comfortable and safe place to live. But opening up to Luc is high risk *and* high reward. He could be the love of your life, Tessa, and you deserve that."

I chew on my lip, nervous and excited, because no one knows me better than these women.

"We don't know if Luc's given up, but I doubt it," Jade says. "You're going to have to find him to get an answer."

"To the right question," I mutter.

"What?"

I wave her away. "Nothing." I pause. "Actually, every-thing. I'm going to Paris."

———

AN EXCRUCIATINGLY LONG TIME LATER, I'M AT A CAFÉ IN PARIS near Luc and Anouk's apartment. Doubts have been creeping in again, but encouraging messages from my friends keep me grounded.

At least, grounded until I spot Luc.

I almost don't recognize him. His shoulders are hunched, his eyes on the ground, worry lines between his eyebrows. He's already passing the café, and I call out his name, standing and weaving my way out of the tables and chairs to chase after him.

"Luc!"

This time he hears me and stops, slowly turning around like he isn't sure what he heard. Our eyes connect, and my worry deepens further.

"Luc, are you—"

The breath whooshes out of me as he takes a stride forward and meets my momentum, wrapping me up in his arms. I've never been so glad to hug anyone in my life, and after the surprise recedes, I return the gesture, wrapping my arms around him. I feel the tension in Luc escape in a rush, and he presses his face into my neck, taking big shuddering breaths that ramp my worry up. *Something* is obviously wrong.

I hold him close and run my hand in a soothing circle over his back. I can feel the struggle in his body to get himself under control, so I add soft, kind words.

Finally, he pulls away, wiping his face with his palms. "Mémé fell yesterday," he explains, and my heart goes out to Anouk, the kind woman who's old enough that a fall could do terrible things. "She's okay now, but she fell, and I wasn't home. I was out driving and had to go back home for something and found her."

"Oh, sweetie," I say. "I am so sorry. Thank god she's okay." I keep touching him, rubbing my hands up and down his upper arms and over his shoulders.

Once he's deemed his face is dry enough, he tugs me toward him again, this time in a simpler hug, a grateful hug, not a collapsing-under-your-stress hug.

Luc places his chin on my head. "How did you find me?"

I laugh against his chest. "I went to your old apartment and knocked on doors until someone called the super so I could get a forwarding address. They probably shouldn't have given it to me, but they did. Then you weren't home, so I thought I'd wait in a café and check every hour. I didn't expect you to walk right by me, though it is on the way to the metro."

He squeezes me once. "Thank you."

"You're welcome." We both pull away, and I catch the look on Luc's face: it's guarded now, unsure, which I've never seen on him before.

"Look, Tessa. With Mémé's injury, I don't know how—"

"Wait," I interrupt. Luc's going to apologize for not being able to come visit me for a while, and I don't want him to feel guilty for another moment. I need to act my age and tell Luc the truth. "I have to ask you a question."

Luc's lips part for a moment before he swallows, his Adam's apple jumping in his throat. "Okay."

"Will you be my boyfriend?"

Surprise bursts from Luc in a laugh. "Really?" he asks, running a hand through his hair.

"Yeah. I know that it's not ideal, being a flight away from each other, and of course, you need to stay here to take care of your grandmother, so I'll come as often as I can. But I like you. A lot. And I know you like me, too. So maybe you can hurry and answer the question."

Luc slips his arms around me and pulls me closer, a winsome smile on his face that has my heart flipping.

"I was going to tell you that even though I won't be able to visit you for a while, I still want you with everything that I have. I was going to ask you to wait for me. I was going to tell you I am obsessed with you." He gives a lengthy pause, searching my face. "That you would come here, worried about me, looking for me. You make me feel so many things, Tessa, and you're all I've wanted."

Part of me still fears this is too fast, too likely to fail. But the other part, one that sounds oddly like my friends' voices, reminds me that Luc's a grown man, and his feelings are his, and I can't control them.

"Really. And I know that it's going to take you longer, but I'm very persistent." I laugh at that. "To answer your question, yes, I want to be your boyfriend."

For the first time, I feel like my smile matches his, open and wide and barely contained on my face. He pulls me into his arms, kissing me soundly as if to reiterate that, if nothing else, he's solid and secure and certain.

We kiss for an inappropriately long time, even for the city of love, and someone eventually jostles us on the sidewalk. Luc pulls back, tugging me with him toward the café.

"Come on, let's get your stuff and figure out how to spend every moment we can together."

EPILOGUE

Tessa

Months later . . .

LUC JOLTS AWAKE NEXT TO ME, MAKING ME SQUEAK AND drawing the attention of several people around us.

"Sorry," I whisper. "Sorry."

Some lady two seats over and one row up huffs at me.

Luc rubs his hands over his face, up into his hair, where he scratches his scalp and blinks at me.

Sorry, he mouths.

It's not his fault, entirely. He took a red-eye to Vienna to spend the weekend with us at the insistence of Jade, Emma, and Sara. This was one of the weekends Luc and I had originally scheduled to spend time together, but when Jade asked if we would come to see her presentation instead, we did some schedule shuffling, and, well . . .

Luc kept his bartending shift last night because he refused to let me pay for the flight. He didn't sleep much last night, and we started early. Jade's presentation began at eight a.m.

However—and I say this with all the love in my heart for my best friend—Jade's presentation is really boring.

Who would have thought that this gregarious, outgoing woman has a horrible public speaking fear and hides behind statistics and studies?

My eyes drift from the presentation slides to the translator. He works at the same company as Jade in the marketing department and is a polyglot. Thus, he's been traveling around the continent with Jade translating her presentations.

This is the guy: the Clark-Kent look-alike Jade has alternatively called Chin Dimple, Superman, or That Asshat, depending on her mood, though his name is Carlos.

He's very attractive. When we first saw them this morning standing together, Sara, Emma, and I all shared a glance with three sets of raised eyebrows. They look good together. He's ruggedly handsome, taller, and Spanish. Jade's skin tone, with her Mexican heritage, is slightly darker than his, and with both of them in black suits walking in together, Jade's streak of white in her ponytail stands out.

Carlos looks just as bored as the audience is, droning on with an echo of Jade's words in German. Most of the audience is Austrian, and while plenty of people here speak English, Jade's company has brought in a mix: some industry professionals, some pharmacists, but also a large contingency of patients, people who traveled from neighboring countries or from more rural areas and are probably not fluent in the technical language Jade uses.

Hell, I don't understand a lot of the stuff Jade is saying *in English*.

For the rest of the presentation, Luc shifts around a lot, trying to stay awake. He leaves his hand on my thigh, the heat of him burning through my jeans. He took a power nap earlier, but it's been two weeks since I've seen him, and I'm definitely ready for some alone time. While Luc didn't let me pay for his flight, I insisted on paying for our hotel room so we could stay together.

To be honest, between visiting my friends and Luc, I'm not staying in my cute apartment all that much. Last month, Anouk traveled to Aix-en-Provence to visit a friend of hers for a week, so I packed up my things and stayed with Luc, working from the small desk in their sitting room.

People start clapping, and I focus my eyes back on Jade, who's got a relieved smile on. The four of us stand and applaud enthusiastically, maybe too loudly to make up for our thoughts.

It also gets everyone else moving, so we'll take it. The crowd ambles to the back of the ballroom, where cocktail tables are set up and displays with information about the various products Jade's company offers.

We head right to the coffee bar.

"Oh my god," Sara hisses while pumping hot water into a mug. "Jade is going to ask us how she did. What on earth are we going to say?"

Emma selects her coffee. "It's okay. We can come up with nice, truthful things."

Luc's hand shoots up. "I call, 'you really know your stuff.'"

Emma, Sara, and I glance at each other. "She looks great," I say.

"The presentation was very legible," Sara suggests.

"Um." Emma contemplates. "The attendance was fantastic?"

Fortunately for us, it's at least an hour before the crowd thins and Jade can find us. She's beaming, and I'm guessing that she enjoys the direct conversations with people way more than giving the presentation. Jade greets Luc with a hug and then sidles up to the rest of us.

"You look fantastic," I say. "Very powerful up there."

Everyone else offers their compliments too, and Jade's

cheeks pinken. "Thanks, y'all. The presentation was good, right?"

There's a beat of silence, and Luc speaks up. "I was very impressed with the numbers." All four of us glare at him, and Luc shifts to slightly behind me and shuts up.

I choose a different tactic. "Are you going to introduce us to Carlos?"

But Jade is not buying it. She puts her hands on her hips, her suit jacket flaring out and her gaze narrowing on us. "Come on y'all. Truth serum."

We all exchange glances. "You did a great job presenting the information," I say.

Jade huffs and glares at me.

"Okay, fine," Sara says, and reaches out to take Jade's hand off her hip. "You know we love you, but it's very obvious that you're nervous when you start, and you bury yourself in the numbers because that's where you're comfortable."

"I'm *presenting the information*."

"Honey," Emma says in a soothing tone. "Truth serum," she says, flinging the words right back at Jade. "You hate this, don't you?"

Poor Jade looks gutted. "I can't hate it. It's a great opportunity. I get to travel, and my boss says this would boost my career." She swallows hard. "You all think my presentation sucks, too?"

"Hang on," I say sharply. "We didn't say it sucks."

"Did someone else tell you it sucks?" Emma asks.

Jade rolls her eyes. "Carlos did."

"He said it sucks?" I raise an eyebrow, having a hard time picturing a professional and grown-ass man telling a woman she sucks at her job.

"No, not exactly." She bites her lip. "He said it was boring."

Okay, well, it's hard to argue with that, but I have half a

mind to confront this man, who I'm *sure* didn't put it kindly at all to Jade based on everything she says about him. That guy has a massive chip on his shoulder, at least when it comes to our Jade.

"It's just that we know you so well, and you have such an interesting story," Sara says. "Maybe you can make it more personal?"

"Yeah. People love hearing great, inspirational stories like yours," Emma adds. "You would give them hope, you know?"

Jade looks off into the distance, thinking, tugging at the end of her ponytail.

"Just think about it," I say. "If you need help, come to us. Now, should we go meet Carlos, or should we go out to lunch?"

Jade opts for lunch, and we look at Sara's list of restaurants with vegan options and pick one. Over our meal, we discuss our plans for the day and cheer Jade up.

"I need a nap," Luc says when Emma suggests seeing The Hofburg. "Sorry."

"Nap," Jade says, lifting an eyebrow. "Or, *nap*." Her eyes slide over to me.

"Both?" Luc glances at me, hopefully.

I reach my hand under the table and squeeze his knee. "Both."

"Ugh," Emma says. "Go be happy and naked together."

I laugh, and Luc winks at me.

We say goodbye and saunter back toward our hotel, Luc's arm slung around me. He leans on me, and then gives me more of his weight, and then he fake-snores in my ear.

"Luc!" I laugh, shoving him off of me.

He grabs me and pulls me even closer, stopping us from walking as he nuzzles into my neck. "I can't help it," he tells me, and he's speaking in French now. "You're so warm and soft and comfortable, and I'm *so* tired."

"I know, my little cabbage," I say, teasing.

Luc lifts his head, and I sift my fingers through his hair, making his eyelid droop in pleasure.

"Thank you for flying here to see me and to support my friends," I whisper.

"You love your friends," he says. "And by extension, they are my friends."

"That is how it works," I say, giggling when I shift my fingers so that my nails scrape his scalp and his eyes fully close.

"Tessa." His forehead comes to rest against mine, and his eyes open, looking down at me with such open affection that it takes my breath away. "I love you."

Warmth radiates out of my heart and fills every cell in my body. This quiet declaration, this romantic gesture, means more to me than any big dramatic gesture.

"I love you, too," I say, and Luc leans in, pressing my body flush with his and sealing our words with a kiss.

I thought Paris was the city of love.

It turns out my city of love is wherever Luc is.

———

THE END

Want one more sexy scene with Luc and Tessa? Sign up for my newsletter for a bonus scene set a few years in the future. Download your copy by scanning here:

Newsletter subscribers also get bonus epilogues and a behind-the-scenes look at the trips that inspired my stories.

Please Review

Reviews are critical to all authors. You can leave a review for *Rosé with My Fake Fiancé* at all retailers

Amazon | Apple | Kobo

Barnes & Noble | Google Books

and

Goodreads | BookBub

Also by Liz Alden

<u>The Love and Wanderlust Series</u>

The Night in Lover's Bay (free prequel short story)

The Fling in Panama

The Slow Burn in Polynesia

The Second Chance in the Mediterranean

The Rival in South Africa (novella)

The Player in New Zealand

The Best Friend in Indonesia (free standalone short story)

<u>Wanderlust Resort Series</u>

Beach Boss (free standalone short story)

Beach Resolution

Put it in Beach Mode

<u>Holiday Retellings Series</u>

Nutcracker with Benefits

Frosty Proximity

<u>Aged Like Fine Wine Series</u>

Rosé with My Fake Fiancé

Riesling with My Roommate

Prosecco with My Professor

Cava with My Colleague

ACKNOWLEDGMENTS

Writing about Tessa and her friends has been such a pleasure. Sometimes I catch myself wondering what my characters would think or do, and I have to remind myself that I am, essentially, them. If you know me, you'll see various parts of my life baked right into the story.

Except I never had a fake fiancé. Ah, well, too late now. I can't demote Captain Alden.

Thank you to my early readers, of which there are many: Lillian Lark, Marty Vee, Sara Whitney, Jordan Bloom, Karen Grey, Cara Dion, and Sara Tallary. I literally could not wait to share this story. I gave it out like candy.

Thank you to my proofreader, Lisa Matsumura, and to Kate Mahon for the amazing cover.

And as always, a big thank you to my husband, who encouraged me so much from day one, and my parents, all five of them, who supported this book in one way or another.

ABOUT LIZ ALDEN

Liz Alden is a digital nomad. Most of the time, she's on her sailboat, but sometimes she's in Texas. She knows exactly how big the world is—having sailed around it—and exactly how small it is, having bumped into friends worldwide. She's been a dishwasher, an engineer, a CEO, and occasionally gets paid to write or sail.

Follow Liz:
Instagram | Facebook | Twitter | Website